THE GODKILLERS HANDBOOK

Kevin W. Smith

CONTENTS

1. Introduction   4
2. Prologue   11
3. The Holy sanitarium   20
4. God has tentacles   29
5. Some irrational catalyst   33
6. The unseen illusion   45
7. Trouble goes wandering   61
8. Church fuckers   65
9. To kill the light   75
10.   Torquemadas vision   78
11.   Lucifers throne   81
12.   The forgone conclusion   92
13.   The Godkillers handbook   94

1 INTRODUCTION

I am not a writer, I do however like to tell stories. The kind of stories you don't hear very often. I am a song writer, a poet, a punk rocker and a trouble maker. I sing and play guitar for a weird punk rock band in Toronto called The Bendecos. This book was an after thought and was written to accompany the album of the same name. This book should come with either a CD or a code to digitally download the album. I originally wrote the lyrics to the album to be a collection of different stories but with a psychiatric hospital as a vessel the story came together. Creatively, this was the toughest, most nerve racking exercise I have ever attempted. The timeline in the story is vague but is happening sometime after the end of the Korean war. This puts us somewhere in the mid to late 50's. I made it up as I went and I think due to my ineptitude for extended prose it makes this book one of a kind and completely original. It could also be complete garbage but I tried.

There have been many concept albums, Rock operas and stage interpretations. I do not think anyone has ever released a "Rock Novel" I can think of a couple of rock operas that would have made more sense to me had there been an actual story told to accompany it. As for the content, I never went to church. I have never been personally wronged in any way by any religious institution. I am not lashing out at God and I do not have any chip on my shoulder about the topic. I simply do not understand Mankind's relationship with spirituality. I do believe in a higher power I just have no idea what it is. I also used a fictional narrator as my actual views on spirituality are now coupled with science. Had I written the book as the actual narrator the summary would have been much different.

I have recently become interested in quantum physics and it answers many questions. Coincidence and premonitions to start, it's a deep subject to tackle but for anyone interested, look up theoretical physics, double slit experiment. The outcome of this experiment may astonish some.

As a result of writing this book I have become completely indifferent towards religion. I am done with it, I have said my piece.

This is due to the fact that churches on a small scale do a lot of good for some. Those who are socially awkward and cannot find a suitable mate may find some comfort in church activities. The elderly who have lost their spouse and are living alone. Addicts that have exhausted every other means of staying sober. I no longer want to think about the abuse of power, the abuse of children, the greed for donations, the division, the wars, the bombings and the never ending crusade for control. I think ones personal beliefs should be just that, personal. Spirituality is not a calling, it is not meant to be shared over dinner. Seems like Tele evangelists, Psychic readers and those claiming to have a connection to the afterlife are for the most part con artists. Saying you have the answers but cannot act on them out of ethics is ridiculous. Tell us where the missing children are Mr. Soothsayer.

It is all religion in question here but Christianity provides the lessons. I wanted to keep it vague and make sure there was an element of embellishment when it came to historical facts. I do not go into the differences of the old and new testaments as that would just require additional history/religious lessons. I easily could have just Googled everything but these historical references are being made in a psychiatric hospital under duress. The basic theme is religion, faith and belief but the human need to belong to something seems to be the focal point. We need acceptance from our peers, our parents and our neighbors. I cant find fault in individuals who have tried other means of social interaction and failed. They tried to find a partner, were not good at sports and seemed awkward in peer groups.

I thought this important to say again as I have tried not to judge anything accept the foundations of power, greed and control. Everyone gets a fair shot with me I don't care who you are or where your'e from. I witnessed prejudice at a young age and understood it well, which in turn brings us to my religion, Punk rock. I discovered punk rock when I was 9. Me and a friend were going through his older sister's record collection looking for songs with profanity. I thought rebellion was great and went from being a Kiss fan to listening to the Sex pistols and Ramones overnight. However, it wasn't for a few years until I fully understood what it was I/we were rebelling against. I was 14 at the local mall with my girlfriend and her mother. While my girlfriend was in a store trying on boots her mother approached me and began to berate me on my appearance. I had been wearing an old leather jacket that was two sizes too big and had a hole in the shoulder. My jeans were ripped, my hair was long and messy. She said how can you go out in public looking that way, aren't you ashamed of the way you look. Do you not look in the mirror before going out, we don't want our daughter dating a slob.

I knew right then and there how bad people feel when having their differences pointed out and ridiculed. Prejudice is wrong, period. On a large scale it's ridiculous, How stupid do you have to be to hate millions of people you have never met? The antithesis of "love thy neighbor?" Promoting hate towards God's creations wont help you much come judgement day. That's one of the reasons music is so important to me. There is nothing wrong with playing music, it's good for the soul. Music is color blind, everyones allowed to be musical. It brings people together, starts friendships and relieves stress. The Bendecos play many different styles of music but in the end it's just loud, fast, rock and roll with some strange themes added in. Our home is in the Toronto underground which is a great community of people. Many of us spent our youth trying to fit in, usually to no avail. There are some who had to hit the streets at an early age due to problems at home. The streets are no place for kids, this is true but in comparison to their home life the streets are sometimes safer. Nothing to lose, nothing to fear. Artificial joy does have a shelf life. When time is up its time to get out. Trading in a habit or addiction for religion is not something I myself would not suggest unless it was a last hope to save you. If it keeps you alive, have at it. Most of us learn early that greed and lust for more is an intolerable trait that must be avoided. Having more wont make your bed more comfortable nor will it gain you loyal friendships.

 Those who could not fit in elsewhere will usually find a home in the underground. Most of us care about animals just as much as humans and don't take well to hearing stories of animal abuse. Punk taught me to ask why and question everything thats unfair and unjust. I try to remain politically indifferent, liberal minded and forward thinking. I have never known a practicing Satan worshipper. The reason you see the Devil or inverted crosses as symbolic sometimes is simple, It pisses off and upsets the mainstream and freaks out the closed minded.

The underlying theme is always the music, it is what brings us together. We all took different paths to get here but we were all walking in the same direction. The sense of community, of belonging to something you know to be absolutely right. Punk rock is the right thing to do but we don't need to declare it. We don't want the rest of the world in on our scenes, we built them for the few not the many. If underground music became popular it would no longer be underground. Punk taught me to accept everyone regardless of nationality, color, class, sexual preference or religious belief. Helping others should be its own reward. I try my best but like a lot of others I feel unworthy at times when I lash out or get angry at something. When I lose my temper and say things I do not mean it hurts.

'No one is perfect that is true but nobody is completely bad either. Until you have walked in someone else's shoes it is unfair to judge someone simply by one act of wrong doing. Isn't this the basic theme of religion? Good and evil, the dark and the light, good from bad, wrong from right. Forgiveness from Whomever, whatever God may be, the great beyond is shrouded from us. Spirituality is within us not in books. What one person may believe may seem outlandish to others. Being a good person should not stem from the fear of bad things happening to us. If you behave poorly around those you are closest to, you may find yourself unwelcome at some point. Religion is becoming obsolete as more and more people are claiming atheist when asked about their faith. So what comes next? Will the complete failure of religion raise ire in our Gods and bring forth the new Messiah? Nobody knows, no one will ever know, but the truth is out there.

We gather once or twice a year east of the city to enjoy a weekend of music, dancing, drinking, smoking etc. Spiderfest, The heaviest show in the universe. This was started by Warren, G Hastings or "Spider" R.I.P. A man who had dedicated his life to punk rock after meeting the Sex pistols in 1976. Spider had been asked to help do sound for the bands first shows. At the time he was a jazz enthusiast working at an accounting firm in the U.K. After witnessing the beginnings of punk rock he had returned to work the following Monday with a zippered leather jacket and dyed hair. He was the same person he had always been yet his friends and co workers shunned him. That was all He needed to see to understand the contradictions and prejudice of society. Just as I had been looked down upon by my girlfriends Mother for the way I dressed, I'm sure Spider felt the same way. Overnight Spider became a punk rocker. At some point spider moved here to the Toronto area and started what was originally called Punkfest. Spider passed away several years now but his legend will live forever. Up until the Covid thing happened the festival was still going strong. Now being overseen by Dan "The Shennan" Aldred, Jay Young and a handful of others. most of which are mentioned in the Thank you. I hope you all like the book, I really hope you dig the album and I welcome any questions, comments or critiques on this project. The bands as well as my personal email addresses will be listed somewhere.

Kevin W. Smith

2 PROLOGUE

Before I get into the origin of this book I want to make something perfectly clear. No one involved with this project wants to kill God.
Nobody hates God.

It's what mankind has done with religion that is in question here.

Lets also be clear that this book does not condemn, ridicule or criticize individual belief. Many people involved with their local Churches or places of worship do so to give back to their communities, help to feed the poor and watch over the elderly. Church going folk are good folk I am sure. That being said, the ideology of the foundations of religion are poisonous and breed self righteous pride and division.

It's because religion is a tool that is used by man to keep the masses moral and under control. Back when social structures were first being implemented four thousand odd Years ago the fear of God seems to be what kept the poor from demanding better lives and stealing from the wealthy.

How many wars have been started due to opposing faiths?

How much hate gets created throughout the world because of which book you read?

The Devil possesses, mad and frantic, something had to be done. If you go back several hundred years, you will find the gradual inception of the middle class. Before that you were either born privileged or you worked the fields farming the back 40.

People literally living dirt poor and the reason you don't complain or go steal bread from the wealthy is divine redemption, thou shalt not steal. Hundreds of years later the middle class was a big part of the caste system, where families worked their share of land hoping their little piece out farms the neighbors.
The problem was you start off with the smallest, least fertile area and have to pay dues to the landowner. Making gains sometimes took a lifetime. The poor were essentially slaving away for their families future while never seeing any profit. Of course Church on Sunday tells you that every man in Heaven is a rich man.

 The middle class were also often wealthy families that either didn't work hard enough or were just unsuccessful in their endeavors, this was also God's will. If you slave in the fields all day every day, refrain from sin, don't question authority or God and never steal then eternity will be yours.

You're also commanded to not bare false witness which came in handy when the poor were asked to inform upon their fellow neighbors. The powers that be want everyone to be the same, to think the same way and follow the same beliefs. This summarization is from An 60+ year old historical text that tries to explain the benefits of being different, thinking different and making up your own mind as to who or what you believe God to be. It was written at a time in history where dissent towards the church was basically unheard of. People probably had no idea of atheism or even realized they could believe in a different origin of life. The mindset back then was to believe what you're taught, do as you're told and never question authority.

 years ago I was given a notebook. At the time, the person who gave it to me made me promise to never tell anyone where I got it from. So names have been changed to protect the guilty and/or paranoid and we will call him "ELI." Reason being, it was obtained during a criminal act which at the time could have tied him to other crimes. It was a notebook containing essays, poetry, historical dates, secret codes, cipher languages, as well as incoherent rants, absurd statements, anti religious hyperbole and vitriolic dissent. I hadn't really read much of it at first but I picked it up again recently and discovered some amazing things. This notebook was the rough copy of a much deeper more sinister piece of literature. Although I am not sure if a final copy was ever completed. The notebook was found in the rafters of an old victorian mental hospital. Eli and his partners in plunder were stripping the building of anything salvageable. They would take copper piping, old medical equipment for stainless steel, wheelchairs etc. These buildings were massive with some impressive architecture. The Holy cross Sanitarium, originally spelled Sanitorium.

The Catholic church built several in the 1920s and 30s to originally deal with Tuberculosis. In the late 40's they discovered a cure with the anti biotic Streptomycin and most of these hospitals that had no use were closed down. By the 50's some of these hospitals became test sites for psychological warfare experiments. This was due to the propaganda used by the Russians after the Korean war. I have no idea which specific hospital the book came from or who the people are who have written in it. After realizing the historical importance of this book I decided I needed more information to fully understand what I was dealing with. I had not heard from "Eli" in years and since I had gotten the green light to translate and rewrite a summary of the book I looked him up. It wasn't hard finding him on social media and figured any type of statute of limitations should have surely run out on theft of a book that no one knows was missing. Or at least that's what I thought.

His reply to me was, "Destroy that book, forget it ever existed" I was blocked from his profile instantly and the next day all trace of him online was gone. He had closed and removed all of his information overnight. I figured this was due to him being in some other kind of legal trouble and didn't want his past crimes brought up. So back to the book I went, 226 pages. a magnifying glass and a graticule for the very small print. This book was really old but had no dates in it and had different handwriting styles but no names. Whomever was writing this wanted to remain unknown and understandably so.

I began researching these hospitals and found there had been many different locations under the scrutiny of humanitarian crimes. Genetic sterilization, deprivation chambers and shock therapy. Some were prosecuted for performing mind control experiments using untested psychotropic narcotics. When Tuberculosis became treatable these mammoth buildings started becoming obsolete. Something had to be done to keep this specific Hospital profitable. Often built far away from urban centers to contain any viral outbreaks and stay out of public view. Medical treatments went completely un-policed. This institution was under the supervision of the Catholic Church, what could possibly go awry in such a place? If you became healthy enough to leave, they found a reason to keep you. At one point the hospital started a campaign to humanely apprehend and incarcerate anyone who may have shown signs of psychosis, psychiatric instability, insanity or even demonic possession. For each patient the hospital received a certain amount of state provided assistance to pay for the cost of care. More patients means more money, although at some point it seems like the patients turned into prisoners. The aged were also rounded up, people were living longer and they claimed that older people became a strain on local doctors needing to make house calls for simple aches and pains. People with epilepsy never left the house after word got out about this.

These hospitals were segregated between the men and women and it seems never did the two groups interact. All the men who had written in the book had been taken to the hospital against their will and it seems like that's where this book originates. They began referring to this act in the book as "god's tentacle." Then at another point a poem about gods tentacle appears in very fine calligraphy and then continues throughout the book every so often. At 80 years old, without a wife or local family to take care of them in times of need, the powers that be deemed them a danger to themselves. The Catholic church then retains the patients estate until being given a clean bill of health. Which at that time probably never happened again. The church took all their possessions, homes and life savings.

However, The men who were writing in this book were extremely intelligent and at that point, collectively vengeful. It seems one man spoke for the rest but there were additions in the book with different handwriting. The summary is translated through the words of one speaking for the group. It seems possible that all involved began by scribbling down ideas or events of the day. It's a few pages in before it becomes written in proper sentence and paragraph form. They must have expanded and summarized after when there was no one watching. From what I could make of it, there were 4 distinct handwriting styles and they often tell their story through we and not I. What's more interesting is that it appears they knew each other prior to being incarcerated together. Possibly as educational faculty, a theoretical physicist, a mathematician, an engineer, a historian, an anthropologist???? It's hard to tell exactly who these men were and if this book was ever completed.

It does go into detail about how they convinced most of the other patients that they were mind reading aliens. They used gestures, signals and vocal sounds to seem to communicate telepathically. The reason for this seemed to be for a means of gathering followers to get everything they wanted. They portrayed themselves as aged wisdom, the elder statesmen of reality and bringers of truth. Possibly as a way to get out, although there is no clear escape plan just different options. It does seem that the patients over 80 were basically left alone making it possible for this group of Godkillers to operate without scrutiny. What harm can a bunch of old codgers playing cards all day do? One thing they seemed to achieve while first writing in the book was they were able to get the word out to citizens in the area that no one was safe from being hauled away. Everyone knew not to get emotional in public and they all kept their medical ailments to themselves. The aged just went into hiding. Children below an I.Q of 50 were no longer welcomed in regular schools and forced to attend differed educational facilities and often forced to leave home to live in handicapped boarding schools.

I eventually read through the whole book page by page. Notes scribbled in the corners, unfinished math equations, religious heresy throughout. Several pages had direct proof of historical inaccuracies and why the truth about the past had to be changed and sometimes completely re-written. Comparisons to the Birth of Christ and how many of the religions of the world had similar origin stories. The more I understood what these men were up to, the more obsessed I became. These men were planning on fighting organized religion, exposing the Catholic church as a monster, a fraud, a brainwashing cult. The question is, on what scale? The book is not all negative though, as there are also positive life lessons here. Aptitude and purpose for anyone willing to listen to them. Did they simply want to prove to the other patients that God does not want them to be locked up there? Were they trying to convince enough of them to overpower the staff and escape? As the book progresses, different options seem to occur to the Godkillers without provocation. The mission in itself may not seem to be the desired outcome. They set out to do the right thing through vengeance. They end up on a path that leads them a little short of their desired location. Or is it? The local citizens all knew to curtail any type of odd behavior and the aged knew they needed to fill beds. Even though the people living in that surrounding area knew what was going on there no one said anything. To be making claims that there was something sinister going on in the sanitarium was crazy talk. If all the information gathered together in this book was properly formatted and organized so that the average person would understand, what would the outcome be? If the facts are placed before the faithful would their dogmatic reality save them from such sac-religious absurdities? Would some actually consider an alternative reason for our existence? Decades after these men accumulated all this data in order to educate and most of the planet still believes in some sort of omnipotent deity. Due to that fact, as best as I can understand it, as best as I can translate, this historical oddity must be told. So Ladies and Gentlemen, believers and non believers, righteous and wretched, blessed and damned. this is the Godkillers handbook.

3 THE HOLY SANITARIUM

Think of us as teachers, we came here from beyond the clouds, from beyond the sun, from light years past the smallest star in the sky. We are a cosmic consciousness manifested into primitive synthetic human form. Summoned here to examine creative artistic expression and then eradicate all trace of your foolish Deity's. We were designed and manufactured to physically mimic your life forms, we are an inter dimensional, galactic collective, bio diverse, human clone cyborg. We will travel deep into the spiritual abyss to drag Jesus back up here to answer some questions. Too lazy to save the world from doom and sin so he lets himself get killed. Then he guilt trips everyone that he died for your sins while telling his earthly followers to beg for money in his name. Thousands of years of depraved indifference, sexual exploitation and holy wars. This planet needs to re discover it's origins. Religion and control with a population bred to worship gold is what brought us to this planet. They lied to you about everything and we have come to correct them. Incarcerating the innocent to pay for their greed was the final act of an abuse of power that has lasted far too long. We can save you! You are prisoners incarcerated for no crime. The God you worshipped your whole life has turned his back on you. Does this all seem a little far fetched? Does it sound crazy? Think about what's in comparison here.

Are you here against your will? Did you or anyone in your family make plans for you to be brought here? Do you want to be here? Is there somewhere safe that you could go to if you were able to leave here? Have you been treated well here? Are you of sound mind? What financial assets{if any} did they obtain from you? Would you like to learn what we can teach you? Will you do everything possible to help us get you out of here?

Can you imagine a different way of life? So unlike the way you live now. An existence without hate and war and greed. That is our infinite task, forever freeing slaves. This reality is upheld by prisoners of a fable that do not realize how easily their freedom can be attained. Don't you people realize that this world you live in has a fundamental belief problem. You are born into a faith, usually handed down from your ancestors. Many are raised to believe that doing wrong in the eyes of those who guard you is somehow defying your faith. So in order to mould children into being what is expected of them they threaten the child with God. Do you feel that God wants you to be kept here against your will? Go tell the Priest that you were talking to God this morning and he told you that he wants you to go back home to live out the rest of your life in peace. It would be considered nonsense and claim you are hearing voices. They will have you drugged and incapacitated in no time. Although it's not absurd for them to tell you what God really wants. They tell you that God wants you here to be kept safe while they take everything you've ever worked for to serve themselves. They are performing sick, illegal medical experiments somewhere in this building and all these patients are lab rats in waiting. Those patients that get taken away then brought back looking like they had seen death itself, is that God? The people here are your

captors not your saviors, they do not want what is best for you. They already have everything they can take from you, if you step out of line, you may disappear with the other lab rats, Does that sound like God?
Do you know about the deprivation rooms? If you misbehave or disagree with what they are teaching you, they lock you up. In a dark room with no outside communication, no sunlight, no way to know what time it is. When you sleep they randomly set off deafening alarms until you cannot sleep at all. If a relative of a patient wanted proof that there was some sort of psychological problem and a reason for them being here. A week in a deprivation room and the right cocktail of sedative narcotics and you have instant crazy. Yes, this place is collective misery and the seeds they are sowing will grow into a poisonous garden of sadness and despair. This place is where faith came to die.

Faith, what a great idea. It probably isn't, but possibly could. It makes sense to have faith, it doesn't cost you anything except a little character and in the small chance you get it right, you win eternity in Heaven. Bible study every day and the only redemption they speak of is death. They cannot preach how Jesus saves or have prayer groups anymore as many of the patients would break down crying asking God why he is keeping them in such a cold and sad place. Why does God believe that hurting me will heal me? You are told that you are broken and need to be fixed. This place is your last chance to make peace with God and let Jesus cleanse you of sin. Behave! Be quiet! Obey! God is watching and the people that run this place are servants of the Lord.

They know him personally and God told them to round up as many innocent people as possible. Take everything they own, Imprison them in this hospital and perform horrifying medical experiments on them. If you stray from his flock, cause any trouble, act unreasonably or question the legitimacy of other faiths, you will be put through electro-shock therapy. Recently there have been many rumors about psychological deprivation experiments. Because God told them to. No one knows what they do to the patients that they take to the far wing of the hospital, it's a big building. But when they come back they are not the same. Content with doing nothing, no apparent mood, no attempt to engage in social contact. They just stare out the window all day. After a while some of them get taken away for good. Sick fucking bastards, destroy their minds in some demented quest for military psychic warfare. Then when they are rendered useless and un responsive they just dispose of them. {The first of the legible poems}

Tortured minds
out to play
there's no reason
locked away
lost and alone
kept here safe
prisoners of god
no hope of escape
Disobedient
basement door
descending cliffs
rocky shores

cinder blocks
neatly stacked
bricks tied tight
to burlap sacks
Vultures circle
for human snacks
Hammer and club
we don't talk back.

Now has anyone actually seen a bundle of burlap sacks tied to cinder blocks out back or was this a fear tactic? Maybe when the unresponsive get taken away its just to a different ward where they can be observed better. They say every time a patient is taken away the vultures that nest in the rock face circle the bay. Waiting in hope that whatever it is that was tossed into the bay eventually floats up for dinner. From the common area the view to the cliff is obscured by the second floor veranda. If someone is being disposed of in this manner it is out of our view. It is true that many seem to go missing when taken out of the common rooms. Vultures had been flying around a lot lately.   Maybe deprivation torture and shock therapy treatment are whats best for these poor lost wretched souls. Lets take a minute to think about that, cold blooded murder. Or if not, the only other reason that type of rumor gets started is if it's deliberate. The back of the hospital is on what they refer to as Aquitaine Bay and is apparently non traversable by any type of sea craft. From the main room windows the view can take your breath away thinking about the drop.

Sick fucking bastards, so lets go through this. Patient is constantly causing problems, does not obey what he is told to do. He is disruptive and loud and continues to verbally assault and pick on other patients. Truth is, He just does not want to be here and is one of the rare ones who are trying to fight for some justice. Or, Patient has been through all the experimenting he could possibly endure. He is in semi comatose, semi vegetative state. He is no longer any use to them. Drugged and knocked out they are wrapped up in a 6 foot wide burlap sack and thrown over the cliff. No pain right? If this is just a scare tactic to keep the patients under control it is still a disgusting trick considering where it's coming from.

As time goes on and as the book is being passed around it becomes all the more evident that the people running that hospital had completely lost all sense of reality. The place seemed to be staffed by some Catholic order of nurses and a few parish Priests. The building operations however seemed to be split. The proper people or Joe Proper and company, military brass, seemed to be the men who showed up only to observe. When patients were lead away to who knows where, they made the Nuns and Nurses do it.
They do eventually come in contact with a younger patient who calls himself the custodian. He claims to have once been a doctor there and during a coffee break he passes on some disturbing stories of inhumane treatment of captivity and torture. How much can they enforce this sick program into you before you break? If you don't break,

congratulations, you're now a soldier? Statements are shared entirety later on in this document. This place seemed more and more sinister by the page.
 What exactly were they doing and how the hell could they be doing it in the name of the Lord? This pit of depravity gets deeper. What are we capable of when we are given power and believe we must abuse it to succeed? The previous establishment was inept at it's core and norms had to be changed. Rules had to be broken. To climb the ladder, to gain social standing, to get things done when others could not. Faced with being shut down, they begin to round up the sick and the aged. If someone went to the parish and had been in conflict with a neighbor, all they had to say is they overheard that person worshipping the devil. As time went by all you would have to do is say is you saw someone talking to themselves or just acting erratically. Bang they would be locked up for temporary observation. Depending on what worth you were to them decided wether you were forced to stay. {The next few pages were filled with meticulously planned bodily gestures, signals, vocal noises, slight of hand tricks and unfinished poetry}

So what they seem to be doing here is creating a network of non traditional forms of communication. This could have been used as a warning system as well as the schematic to fool the other patients. For an example it starts out with a chart using simple signals.

SIGN	RESPONSE	PURPOSE
left shoulder shrug	quickly move out of view	telepathy/early warning
left eye rub	appear quickly	Diversion/ break up dialogue
right eye rub	coast is clear/continue	move un noticed/ avoid security

There are 3 full pages of these charts, they had their own sign language. There was also whistling, stamping feet and one word signals, What genius, the patient would have been in awe after witnessing this, the doctors, Clergy and staff had no idea. They must have been a quiet group of old Coots as they did seem to stay out of trouble, under the radar and away from the deprivation rooms. Or did they? there was another short piece of writing.

Today's yesterday is not the same as yesterday's yesterday
Tomorrow's yesterday will not be today
yesterday's tomorrow will.

There is more of this type of thing as the book goes on but it may suggest that the deprivation rooms may not have been just for unruly patients. This may have been another mind control test or deprivation to see who would last the longest. Why the need to be able to stay one step ahead of everyone? Seriously? mind reading robots? At least three of the men writing in this book were over the age of 80. They all have their own stories of waking up tied down or not knowing how they got here. There is some very cerebral and meaningful essays about spirituality, God, Satan, Prison, war, redemption and much stranger topics arose as time went by. So had

one or all of them just gotten to the hospital or had
one or all of them just obtained this book?

4. God has tentacles Dunstal Clarke and Emery Wane

Full names are not often mentioned in the book but this rare occasion is one of the more interesting side stories. Apparently these two retired butlers had been so sickened by the decadence and depravity of the upper class that they decided on spending their final days, along with their pensions, getting drunk with the homeless.

They must have been hero's supplying booze for downtown hobo's and transients. They ended up getting away from the dumpster filled alley's and camped out down by the train station. They must have realized their pensions would go a lot farther with just the two of them. They sat at the top of a hill behind some brush, watching the trains pulling in and out of the station. Then one summer it had rained for three days on and off, the ground was saturated. Wane and Clarke were both retirees and probably around 75 years old, they could not make it up the hill but they tried. No one knows exactly how it happened because both of them were drunk but Emery lost one leg, Dunstal lost both. Their camp was getting blown away along with their stash of money and booze. They say they never heard the train coming, there are always horns sounding and train car connections slamming together where they camped. They had tried several times to get up the hill through inches of wet mud and probably passed out at the foot of the hill where only the oil tanker cars are parked. One train conductor said earlier on they were covered in muck rolling around on the ground laughing. To their luck a prostitute named Iris happened to be looking for them.

The two men had helped out many times when she was in need. Iris somehow made it to the station and was able to get some paramedics to the men before they died. They believe that it was an angel of the lord who came down to save them that night. They both say that the lord offered them a second chance if they cleaned up their act and they did not. They in turn took their wheelchairs to the bank, got their booze and then right back to the tracks. Then karma shows up With God's tentacles and serves them their redemption. Old men, no fixed address, alcoholic vagrants, eye sore to passersby. They had targets on their back and days after they got here they were born again. Now they preach, they repeat their story of divine intervention over and over and deliver sermons to anyone disrespecting the good book. They would not stand for the God's tentacle metaphor, they were incarcerated for their sins and only alive because Jesus died for ours. Because the two have become such religious zealots, they attracted the ire of our little group of Godkillers. In return we give it right back, they start warning us about saying bad things about the lord, so we whisper "God has tentacles" when they walk by.

The sad and sorry story of Dunstal Clarke and Emery Wane
One lost a leg the other lost both, dancing with a train.
Atop a slippery hill in pitch dark pouring rain.
Both survived both went insane.
An angel of mercy appeared before them that night,

saved them on condition they clean up and live right,
their idea of living right drinking every drop in sight,
God came back to collect, they didn't put up a fight.

Rumors of eternity draws their ear
We keep busy tempting the weak, we are something to
fear
This place not friendly to the aged, we may destroy you
next year
When morning does strike and turn back into night,
Contested by millions of tears.

Not friendly to the old
the silence of the moon, stills your soul,
voices in the shadows best bite your tongue
We are the ancient, sent to destroy the young.

Come with us Clarke and Wane
forget about god, forget about the train,
to defy our mission would be a fresh new damnation,
there have been many before, but we will be the last,
We were not here yesterday but we were here for
creations past
And as time slowly erases us we become more
disdainful of this task.
We hold this key, condemned to all eternity
We have witnessed the re born soul of your God
He will not be forgiving to those who have enslaved in
his name
damnation to all with a wink and a nod.

God has tentacles but he's not an Octopus

*He beats up prostitutes, he's always sleeping on the
bus,*
God has tentacles, his teeth are green and cracked,
He lies about his age he's trying to forget his past.

The thing that really makes this interesting is the two old men absolutely believed what we were telling them. No regular human could get away with saying God has tentacles and beats up prostitutes without being struck down by a bolt of holy lightning. Not to mention, no one else in this place would ever say these things, no normal person would. It all ends up the question of sanity and reality. Are we insane or are we telling the truth. We must be alien robots, not to mention we had the two of them completely disturbed when we first tried the telepathy tricks on them. We knew everything before it happened, we can summon each other and read the minds of the weak. This is a great way to gain trust by telling certain patients they must be very head strong and intelligent because we cant get through. Once we had their full attention we could then show them the truth to what was going on. Sooner or later word had to get through to someone who would dare send some sort of authority to investigate swirling rumors. If not we have one other back up plan that just might just set things right.

AA

5 SOME IRRATIONAL CATALYST

The next part of the book seems to focus on keeping an open mind when being introduced to something unfamiliar. It also examines why we are drawn to things that may not be good for us, and the importance of following these interests anyway. If you don't try it, how do you know you wont like it? The substance of content here seems to be gradually but deliberately written to get people to at least consider alternative reasons for our existence. The following is meant to be a catalyst.

Belief, hope, faith, desire, need, love, infatuation,acceptance, connection, union.

Familiarity, complacency, doubt, fear, suspicion, contempt, anger, regret, separation.

A new process of belief. A way to look at life through a different point of view. If something peaks your interest then at least inquire as to what the substance of that interest may be. You have a world of choices as to how to spend your time. It is the process that should be emphasized here not just picking out a new hobby at a craft store.

Why is it, that things that we are drawn to automatically will sometimes end up pushing us away? What is it that brings on these certain interests? More importantly, why is it we can also be so easily turned off at the same interests over time? Some interests such as a favorite sports team, favorite singer/performer or artistic interests can last a lifetime. However it isn't unreal to move to a new city and follow a new sports team. Some may follow two or more favorite teams. Artistic and career interests may change with age as well as peers and environment. People feel they have outgrown certain things or have matured.

The process of constantly keeping an open mind, welcome change and do not criticize or fear things that you do not understand. Of course when it comes to the human connection it's usually best to not consider everyone you may feel physically attracted to. Love and hate and all the grey area in between. We become attracted to someone we feel will be a good match for ourselves. We can also become over the top infatuated at first sight. Superficial or not, there is no reasoning with us when we are emotionally enveloped by someone. Years can pass after relationships have ended where one or both involved still has an emotional attachment. In other cases, what seemed as the greatest possible partner turns sour overnight.

Treat others as you wish to be treated yet those we love the most are quite often the ones we hurt the most. It seems best to forgive and forget when being slighted by someone but seems a far cry from the norm. Is it so hard to say? "I really want to be with you and I will do whatever it takes to make this work. So please let me know if I start doing things that really turn you off or upset you." Sometimes we blame and lash out when we are separated from a partner. Someone we once cared for and loved becomes the enemy overnight and our faith in love and relationships becomes jaded.

The belief that staying together for the kids is also wrong. Living in tension, sarcasm and insult is never good for the children. While most would agree, it's far better being raised in a traditional Mother/Father home than a broken one. However where should we draw the line when a child is being raised in a war zone?
People do seem to have soul mates. Often the person we meet or know who compliments our own lifestyles the best. Once again there's different shades of grey here, as we have all heard that opposites attract, regardless of how the relationship gets resolved. Then occasionally there is the irrational catalyst that no one can explain. Love at first sight that never dies even after separation

Being a natural at a certain task, such as a sport or art etc. Something you knew the first time trying you were going to be interested or you automatically excelled at it. Something that stays with you forever regardless of time and distance spent apart. We should always be searching for enlightenment. We should always initiate connections that may lead to opportunities to learn new things. However, there doesn't seem to be much grey area when it comes to religion in this matter. Those born into faith based families either seem to be devout followers their whole life or will rebel against whichever denomination they had been forced into.
 Are those drawn into religious circles just looking for somewhere to belong when all else has failed? The people working in this hospital have a calling to help people. Either through the word of the lord or for medical treatment. Most of the staff that take care of the patients in the main building here are not involved with what goes

on at the far wing of the building. However, they do know damn well that there are terrible things happening there. They are also present when unruly patients are given shock treatment to calm them down. They are also witness to the deprivation rooms. Sworn to keep those in their care out of harm.

Sworn to spread the good will of the lord. They are taught to believe that these people are mentally as well as morally ill and need to be dealt with in the strictest of measures if there is any chance in saving their soul. Without their care, who would comfort those patients in distress? Are these Nurses and Nuns wishing they had a different calling? So with indirect threats looming over anyone who might think of exposing the cruelty in that hospital, no one ever says a thing. It is this way because it is.

At some time during everyones life we are introduced to something that immediately grabs hold of us. For some its an art or hobby, others it could be playing sports or a career to follow. Point being, everybody has some sort of aptitude that they can apply to their everyday lives. However, practicing in things that are not common to the general populace may raise some ire in those with authority. I'm not going to go into detailed description of what may be considered perverse, immoral or illegal. As long as you're not hurting anyone or yourself, have at it. What is important here is that, why just be good at something if you can be great. What is it about you that makes you special? This will be an underlying theme throughout this book and it may be be a useful question.

They could have been building their own little army of the willing. If so, this may have been dangerous

considering them not knowing who was actually mentally unstable and who could have alerted the staff someone was promoting dissent. However, getting as many patients as possible all doing something different would be a perfect starting point to what the long term plan was. They wrote short, anecdotal essays explaining why it was so important to follow your interests undauntedly.

When you lie in bed at night, what is it that calls out to you? When everything in your life is bringing you down, what do you indulge in to calm the storm? If you have to get up to go to work everyday and not have some sort of stress relief it will bring you down. The importance of that gear in the mind that starts to race when triggered. Something to achieve, it doesn't have to impress anyone but yourself but why not set out to impress everyone? For some reason we look at each others achievements in awe just because we are unable to do the same. Fact is, if you love to do what you do, you're eventually going to get good at it. There is always more to do, more to learn, more to create. Why is this important? First of all, our favorite things are what make us happy. When we are guided away from them and have different activities forced upon us it breeds resentment. We then grow up to force our interests on our children and so forth. Another reason to let talents flourish is to extend and create new ideas to the world.

What if everybody just painted bowls of fruit? Being locked up in this hospital is like painting a bowl of fruit. Same thing every day, medicated to their satisfaction and told what to do. Forced to listen to the lessons they want to teach you and not given the freedom to question them. Mouse keeps getting away from the trap with the cheese, I think it's time to build a better mouse trap. This is a situation that guided creativity by purpose and demand. Does this serve the creator as an artistic expression even if he was commissioned to make the trap? Does it matter?

If the person building the trap lays in bed thinking about a practical new way to create something no one has ever seen before, its a grand accomplishment. Everyone needs to be encouraged to do what they love to do. They also must be allowed to do it differently than what everyone else is doing. So lets imagine an art class with 20 students. The teacher says I'd like you to paint a bowl of fruit. Teacher does not say you must paint a bowl of fruit. 19 students paint a bowl of fruit, the one other uses pastels to draw two ducks on a pond below a valley. This does not necessarily mean they were meant to be an artist but that person for that instant was a teacher. Everyone of the other 19 students wished they had thought of that and everyone of them will remember that lesson. It's good for the soul to do something new that no one has ever thought of and yet for the most part life is monotony. Wake up, go to work, come home, eat, drink, sleep, repeat. That is why creating new things is so important. Whatever the catalyst is, when something grabs ahold of you and makes you completely fulfilled it removes negativity. People must be allowed to follow their interests or it will eat away at them. Voices in the middle of the night calling you, asking why you were not doing what you should. Why were you not there to do what you needed to do to give you that little piece of satisfaction? Something to be proud of when you feel unworthy. The thing you rush home to after a bad day. How do we get to a point where one person paints a bowl of fruit and the other nineteen create completely different works of art?

You can also fill this need with drug or alcohol use and abuse. People with addictions that have access to their drug of choice are often able to function in society. Creative and intellectual release can go hand in hand with artificial joy but will not last forever. The creative outlet can be easily but temporarily replaced. A dart player down at his favorite pub becomes a local champ. He believes that always having a few pints of beer in him was the trick. Even though alcohol removes coordination his brain adjusted to seeing through impaired eyes. Came the night of the championship final, our protagonist is no longer playing at his pub with his buddies standing behind him. Believing it was beer that got him there he starts putting them back. Does he win? does it matter. What did he believe in? the great game of darts? Himself and his recent achievements? Beer, because it had never let him down before? Is there a similarity to religion here? What was the part that fulfilled him, accolades for sport, drinking away the stress of daily life or being accepted in a social circle that he previously may have thought unworthy of?

Self worth helps us climb the hill and if it is through drugs or alcohol in moderation then have at it. If it is the one and only thing you think of at night in bed, or at work all day, then it alone fills that space for you. It alone will show in your eyes and everything else will become secondary. People constantly getting fucked up for too long often find themselves getting fucked over and taken advantage of. It never comes for free. The art student creates some great works and receives a grant to continue. Art becomes commerce and he goes back to painting bowls of fruit. It's hard to trade a habit, the thing that called out to you in the middle of the night wants to stay by your side. After extended exposure to this habitual activity, do you still want to keep it by your side? After extended periods without your habit, do you want it back? Do you need it back?

Can you survive without it? Do you want to survive without it? The ambitious will fill their time with many different leisure activities, hobbies, sports, clubs etc. However there is always a catalyst that draws them into it. No matter how strange, how different or against the grain something may be, the world would be a better place if these things were accepted instead of silenced and labelled insane or heresy.

As irrational as it may seem, some of us will run straight into things that have been deemed, dangerous, illegal, immoral, or just plain different. The catalyst being it's something most normal people wouldn't do so we gotta try it. Forward thinking in every sense makes sense. If we weren't constantly trying something new we would become complacent and stale like religion. So why is it that organized faith seems afraid of change? Because with change comes truth and a child coming of age in a religious environment will eventually ask the question. Why are there other Gods? Why does it say to love everyone but man shall worship no other idols? So in some instances we get told that God has put other Deity's and religions before us in order to test our faith. So what does that lead to, we must love everything that God has created. So we must love other religions but we cant accept them? God is everything, he is everywhere he loves everyone, he just wants you to avoid a few books. What about the Born again Christian who gives everything he owns, his time, his money and his soul to God after he receives a sign from Jesus that seems to get himself out of certain doom? He prayed and his prayers were answered. He changes his life and gives all his spare time to the Church. Then some terrible accident kills those he loves most. What is this poor guy going to think now? God extended his hand to him when he needed help but took everything he loved away from him right after.

These lessons also state that when relying on that catalyst to get up the hill you best make sure you can get up the hill without it. The distant voices that tend to stay by your side get louder when unanswered. Whatever you do to answer those voices becomes habit. One of the reasons I believe our religions get forced upon us is that there is no or very little calling to give up the rest of your life to serve a God that you have no interest in. There is satisfaction in creating art, designing a better mouse trap, the first taste of the day of your drug of choice. These are things our mind draws us into. So why are we not more interested in this amazing story about an all powerful supreme being? God, or how his only son, Jesus gets betrayed by those he helped yet forgives them. He gets murdered through a slow torture of bleeding out while being nailed to a big piece of wood. The son of God, not one person thought that it might be good for the soul to save him. We don't need ridiculous fictional tales to understand the correct paths in life to follow.

The collective outcomes of most of the worlds holy scriptures can easily be replaced by a few pages. We don't need hundreds of pages to tell us that helping others is a good thing. Even if you only help others with the thought of getting something in return or financial gain, if those you help are unaware of this at the time is there harm done? If you come out and say that you would like to help as long as the favor is returned in some way, no harm done. If you like to help because it gives you some self worth, you like telling people about all the charities you spend your time on. Is there anything wrong with that? Let them brag if they need to, as long as the children get fed and those in need are taken care of, mission accomplished. Helping each other out should just be automatic not a form of judging ones self worth. Helping others is a good thing, it should be echoed throughout the world.

So how do we get to that place? The most irrational catalyst when it comes to human behavior is love. How great it can be when a whole group of people come together for a common good. Yet love between two people who don't have the same beliefs can be a problem. Faith in particular often determines who you should marry. This trend has changed somewhat but in fundamentalist situations you must marry into faith.

Another question is why does love so often breed contempt? Two people who have decided they no longer wish to be together vary rarely walk away as friends. Yet at the beginning the two can not keep their hands off each other. Our minds seem to need some form of re assurance that it was other persons fault the connection failed. Although never assume you're with the wrong person if something attracted you to them. They are there because of our instinct to find the right person to be with. It may all go up in flames but will you regret not taking the initiative when you feel someone is sending you signals? If we try to react to as many catalysts as possible will opportunities arise more often? You can't fail all the time. This is some universal form of dissent that has changed names and supported different causes. This is not advising anyone to do anything reckless or dangerous, it's simply asking people to always keep an open mind. Condemning the unknown is not productive. Until you meet God, he can be anything you want him to be. You are allowed to believe in whatever you want to. If you get it wrong do you really think there will be eternal damnation?

I sometimes get the feeling I am inviting the devil into my life but not evil as we think of it. Some see the devil as a source and sign of freedom. Not having any rules and living your life just being judged by the way to treat and receive people. No church on Sunday, no faith to contemplate, no religious beliefs but maybe still deeply spiritual. In a sense that wonder replaces faith and we hope there is something up there? Out there? Maybe whoever created all this got bored and is now living in a burned out car in an empty field. Our creative endeavor here metaphorically feels like we have raised the devils interest and he knows where we are. However there is a latch on the gate that he can not figure out. It's called the curse of St. Peter

6   THE UNSEEN ILLUSION

The next part of the book focuses on history, reality and truth. It also deals with inaccuracies, exaggerations, plagiarism and contradictions. There was either many hours of research done here or the collective knowledge of these men is really impressive. Once again there are a few different handwriting styles scattered but summarized by our main translator, all following the same narrative. Scripted in lesson form and in simplicity, to teach all that were willing to learn. It begins with his bizarre story of how he ended up there.

With an 80th birthday approaching, I had become ever so worried that I would soon be taken away. One of my biggest mistakes was talking about these fears openly. The authorities in that area had started a reward program for anyone pointing out those with mental instabilities, severe medical issues or religious heretics. Demonic possession was a common belief that seemed to stem from the old Salem witch trials. They also claimed that anyone living past the age of 80 would be a danger to themselves if living alone. They said we would get sick and have accidents much more often and needed constant care. Well I was healthy, sane and had started going to church regularly because those frequently absent were often pegged as anti-Christian or even Satan worshippers.

I was well known in town and served a purpose here for many years although we cannot go into my family name as I wish to keep following generations out of this.

I spoke too much, I confided in those I should not have and as a result of that they took me away.

Most of the octogenarians that are brought here get ambushed at their doctors office, first visit after turning 80. Well I made damn sure to keep healthy and stay as far away from anyone with authority as possible. I asked neighbors to keep an eye out for anything suspicious during the day. I paid a few Ladies of the evening to do the same for me at night. In the end I was taken away for the reason of paranoia. They were unaware I had long passed my 80th birthday. Weeks earlier I had run a rope out my back window that lead out to the alleyway. Another 100 feet added on brought it within steps of where my new prostitute friends did their business. I had the rope on my end attached to a small bell that if rung would be loud enough to wake me up but no one else. There were 2 different types of ambulances in town and the prostitutes on the corner were well aware of the one that came from the sanitarium. The hospital ambulances travelled alone with 2 paramedics and occasionally a physician. The Holy cross ambulance was always accompanied by a police car and there was usually a member of the clergy present. My lady friends had become very fond of me at this point as every day on my way home I would stop and give them what spare change I had on me. They kept an eye out for the ambulance and knew exactly where the rope was if it was sighted.

The plan was, that if they did see some sort of suspicious authority entering that part of town to quickly pull the rope a few times and rush over to the back of the house. I was then going to sneak out the back disguised in a younger mans attire and a hood. They would then hide me in their quarters until I could safely get out of town and on a train to who knows where. I had only my most personal belongings packed up, I had taken most of my life savings out of the bank but not all, I left a small amount to avoid alerting anyone of my departure. I was just going to get on a train and leave everything I have ever known because of my suspicions. I should have just packed up, sold the house and left a year ago when all these strange things started happening. Where would I go anyway, I am almost at the point that I will soon need medical attention, although I wont go into my personal afflictions? I also considered the fact that I knew one of my closest colleagues was already in the sanitarium and I was sure the remaining few friends of mine would end up there shortly. Still, I would have risked the escape. I had confided in my neighbors about my worries and that was my big mistake. I guess having an escape plan to avoid being kidnapped and drugged by the church in the middle of the night sounded crazy to them.

The night they came for me, they surrounded my house. I was supposedly a crazy, paranoid old man who had lost his grip on reality. There was no telling what I was capable of and my previous good standing reputation in the community now meant nothing. I remember hearing screaming just before the bell first sounded. The authorities knew about the rope so they sent a priest with 2 policemen down the back alley. The screaming I heard at the beginning was the 3 men throwing the girls on the ground as they made their way to the rope. Any escape would have been futile at that point anyway. As I first looked out my back window I saw the priest bent down over one of the ladies berating her with religious hyperbole. The poor girls mouth was covered in blood, she was crying begging to be helped up. The priest pushed her head back down and hollered "On your knees before a servant of the lord you wicked heathen, you are a mockery to all that is righteous and pure. How dare you attempt to interfere with the work of the lord?" The other women began helping her up and as they got her to her feet one of them shouted at them that they wouldn't let them take me. The police then raised their batons and charged towards the group of women. I thought they were going to kill them. After several attempts at yelling down to them they finally noticed me and I agreed to go quietly as long as no harm would come to the ladies.

They drugged me and strapped me down anyway, I guess for the optics of it all. I found it odd, I worried that they would take me away because of my age. Then they took me away because I was worried {paranoid} that they would take me away. Because of my former career, my social stature meant as long as I was healthy I was hands off, I was not to be treated unfairly by the powers that be. Which I am guessing means it would have kept me out of the Sanitarium. I had told a couple different neighbors about the elderly being taken out of their doctors offices and sometimes their homes to be locked up and experimented on. I had shown them the rope. In the end I was absolutely right in the fact that I knew they would come for me. I was right to be worried. Now in their eyes I guess paranoia may be evident. I was telling people that I was worried about being abducted out of my own home by authority of the church. I was thinking about running away, I made an escape plan, had a disguise, a warning bell and paid some prostitutes to protect me. I guess it sounded like I was paranoid. So I am here not because of my age and health but because I was worried that I may end up here. I was paranoid that they thought I was paranoid.

Now that I am here, Do I just put up and shut up and be a good prisoner or should some discourse serve my ego and pride? It wasn't long before finding that old colleague who had the same thoughts of self serving revenge. We sought out a few others who still seemed in full control of all their faculty's but also irate at the fact they had been deemed unfit for society. In the eyes of those running the hospital we were insignificant. We decided that, in order to remain harmless to them, we act slower, weaker and content. I found out us octogenarians were not as closely monitored as the rest of the patients so behind close doors our scheme began. It was obvious as to what we were opposed to, our captors, the servants of the lord, the decay of humanity, the source of suffering, the departure of reason, This house of God. Who are these people deceiving apart from themselves? Surely they cant be wholly dogmatic to every word of the scriptures. They would have to figure themselves doomed to hell for what goes on here under their supervision. Imposters, hypocrites, thieves, liars.

The assets that the church seized from our collective estates was a small fortune. We have all been told our savings and property pay for our care and what's left has only been frozen until we are deemed capable and able to be released from this place. We unfortunately all outlived our wives and have no family locally that could request our release. The bigger problem here is, once they know someone may come under review for release, they make sure you are unable to be released. Most of us learn quickly that you do not want to be removed from the common areas for any reason. We play stupid, confused, meek but at the same time we don't want them thinking any of us are becoming overly needy or in need of extra care. Those who have lost any control of their bodily functions get taken away. Those with early onset dementia don't last long either. Put it this way, if you make their work any kind of problem, if they have to get dirty cleaning up after you, you go to the other side. Exposing this place was becoming an obsession, fixation, frustration, If I give in do I reap salvation? This may seem aimless but at least it gives us something to do. Something to achieve, to give us inspiration to keep going and stay alive, safe and healthy. To expose this place, to prove the irrational redundancy of religion. Theology for the simple man, forced belief, the ideology of control and power, light for the blind. They think they know something the rest of us do not. There is no more time for confession, it is pointless now, God is not listening.

I do believe in a greater, higher consciousness. The truth to our existence must be either far too complicated for us to reason with or it is something so terrible they had to make up a ridiculous, complex story. A ghost from the man in the clouds came down to earth, secretly impregnated a virgin without her knowing and then tormented and confused the son throughout his life only to be murdered quite easily by us humans that he came down to save. Well bless me and save my indifferent soul because I will play the game. It keeps me awake at night, I have late hour breakdowns that fill me with despair because it seems so easy to just live free without restrictions and rules. To treat every person equal regardless of nationality, color, class or belief. We were always free, these things that have enslaved us were merely ideas.

I lay awake thinking, if the rest of the world actually understood the history of mankind's relationships with the afterlife, would it free us? As far as we know there hasn't been a deity interacting with man in over 2000 years. So were going to go through this and even though I believe I am doing this for the future of man I often feel like I am actually driving the stake myself. What if knowing religion was a sham from the beginning becomes a killing mistake? What if those who have given their whole lives to faith now have nothing to pray to? God's are jealous? yes they sure are but due to the circumstances that have imprisoned us there are facts that must be shared to all willing to listen.

Throughout the world, there are many different religions with many different Gods. This in it's simplicity should raise doubt in those who are not even geared towards spirituality. Yet we have burdened ourselves with faith. Yes there seem to be many different Gods, but thats because your God of choice is testing your faith. Whats even more baffling are the overlapping religions, such as Christians and Jews who believe parts of the same story but stand in complete opposition to other parts. Jews don't like the sequel to the first book. God is jealous, even though God created that in which he could oppose. Even though God created man in his image and bestowed a constantly learning and changing mind in us. This text will not copy passages from the main religious testaments of this world. The Bible, Quran etc Those books are filled with contradictions that get deliberately overlooked or just plain ignored. Translating and debating those scriptures would be an endless endeavor. What we aim to do, is point to the facts and where to educate people in these matters. There are a few different Biblical passages that we will go over as they have relevance to the situation. However nothing will be quoted, we can give you the basics as to understanding in present terms. We can start with the redundancy of a jealous God. Yes, the all knowing creator of everything gets jealous. The golden calf story with a modern delivery. Moses went up Mount Sinai to deal with some really heavy business. Tells the Israelites he will be back in 40 days with the word of God, so they waited. After what must have seemed like 39 days, they get bored and decide on creating their own God. They somehow find thousands of golden ear rings, melt them down and turn it into a bull calf.

Then for some reason they begin to idolize the gold calf and in turn have a big party worshipping all that is cow. Moses finally shows up with all these rules and tries to break up the cow party. Moses hears a noise that sounds like a war was beginning but it was the sound of the singing and dancing around their new lord Apis the bull calf God. Moses throws a tantrum, they had a party without him, breaks the huge rocks that had all the new rules. God also freaks out, plans on unleashing a killing spree but instead tells Moses to enlist a group of abstainers and morally superior believers that were known as the Tribe of Levi to gather up all their weapons march right into the gold bull party and slaughter them all.

 Like I said thats embellished and over exaggerated but you can go do the research yourself, thats basically how the story goes. All of this to prove that no matter what you do in life you must not idolize anyone but this God. So before we rip this story apart lets briefly examine the position of dogma. The unquestionably true assumptions of holy infallibility. If it is written it is true, the word of the lord must be obeyed. If the people here are true Christians than wouldn't they be thinking that they are on their way straight to Hell when this is all over. Jealous and paranoid, the omnipotent landlord of the universe just cant stand losing. Whatever the truth to our existence is, it must be some kind of horrible meaning for mankind to create such an unbelievable fictitious story. Those at the top know the truth, our purpose has been twisted into freewill slavery. The reality we don't get was once for sale. You could buy the truth and move into the enlightened class but no more. It's been kept hidden throughout the ages. If this illusion of religion were ever taken away from the faithful we would be left with science and proof. Which should lead us to believe that our origins, our purpose, our meaning must be so horrific and convoluted. It must be way to much for the simple man to understand. The horror of reality would render us all insane. So best get on with your struggle and disregard all notion of divine interventions.

I suggest trying as hard as you can to accomplish something that will place you in a position of comfort. Forget praying for inner peace, I do not think eternity is in our best interest's now. Just surviving long enough to channel my ambition into the rest of this text. We are here because the truth is buried out there. Holy men and women left in a position to play God. I believe the illusion is about to break. The veil they use with God and hospital to claim essential needs has become a farce. This place is the looney bin and everyone for miles around knows it. Doctors that fix the brain from the outside are not always taken that seriously in society. It seemed easy to hire more psychiatrists as the patient numbers grew. We were summoned by God to come live as the rest of his flock lives. To be taught false hope in order to be maintained. I hope someday soon this book wont even be needed and people will just learn enough on their own that leading a good life and treating people with respect should not be disposition due to the fear of consequences. What do they say in prayer? Do they ask forgiveness for sending a patient to shock therapy because of erratic behavior and later find out it was a food allergy? He had started waving his arms trying to speak to the nurse but his tongue and throat were swollen and he could hardly breathe. They gave him electric shock for over 30 seconds until his face began to swell up and turn blue, then red. He lived through hell and went over 2 minutes without oxygen and survived. Although he is now blind and can barely form sentences when speaking. He just lays in bed all day now.

These people are sworn to do good, if you want to tell a young child what it is a religious figure does, that's a good start. His job is to do good, but not in this place, they are Shepard's we are sheep. There were still many rooms to fill. I mean, the doctors take an oath to keep their patients out of harms way at all costs. The atrocities that are happening will soon be noticed by someone. Somethings got to give here, there are two many middle aged men returning in vegetative states or sometimes worse. Experiments on the criminally insane was just the beginning. So we are here locked up in a growing society of the wretched, the weak, the aged and the broken.
 The folks that run this place are playing deadly games with the less fortunate, all in the name of a jealous God. If God created everything and is in everyone, how the hell can he be jealous of that which he created? These Israelites had just been freed from Egyptian slavery but somehow had enough gold to make a bull calf? What did they melt the gold in? Aaron throws all the ear rings and trinkets into the fire and a bull comes out? Maybe they found a big foundry pot in the bushes. Then the story

goes as far as blaming the whole thing on these Erav Rav people. Apparently some of these folks were magic and were the ones who started the party. Regardless of who started it, they were all murdered in cold blood, 3000 men, women and children. For singing and dancing around a gold statue. True Christians believe these stories, word for word. God is good?

 I have over the years been told there are subsequent teachings that say the passages in the bible are just anecdotal metaphors designed to teach us right from wrong in a basic sense. However, when following a religion based on faith and dogma, it all becomes someone else's rules and beliefs, not the person who maybe is just looking for answers. This becomes very confusing when growing up and realizing there are many things that just don't make sense. You are not to question what you have learned, if it is written it is true. So some grow to think that maybe it is all anecdotal. God asks this guy named Abraham to bring his only Son Isaac up a mountain and sacrifice him to prove his faith in the Lord. Then, at the last second God tells him he was only joking. God was just testing Abrahams faith here and Abraham was prepared to kill his Son. This story is beyond absurd. First of all, what would have happened if Abraham refused? I suppose God would have killed them both and sent them straight to hell? What would Isaac think? He now spends the rest of his life knowing his Father was prepared to murder him. Now if God was so great, You would think he would have let Isaac in on the joke ahead of time. Or if Abraham refused I would have guessed that God would have said, great, yeah don't be killing your Son because you hear voices in your head.

  Even as anecdote, people think there was nothing wrong with believing in these teachings. Just reading the good book makes you an upstanding, law abiding, God fearing person. That's fine but the ignorance goes with it does nothing to help these law abiding citizens now locked up by their own God. Whatever any given individual believes, the people at the top demand that every word they say be followed without question. Every story, every word is true, as far fetched as it may seem. Past history of the Norse, Greek, Roman Gods etc, turned into mythology over the years. Considering these mythologies all had several different Gods, the over lapping origins and names might have been partial reason to declare the "One and only God" religions. Which leads us to examine the origin contradictions.

We all know the basics to the birth of Jesus. The ghost of an omnipotent all knowing deity becomes bored with controlling eternity and decides he wants to have a son. He somehow manages to impregnate a virgin without even meeting her and without her knowledge of the conception happening. This leads us to the the Nativity scene, where the only son of God is born in a barn amongst farm animals. Three kings were able to follow a really bright star exactly to the very spot the birth occurred. One of them had gold, the other two, although being kings, only happened to have incense and some kind of ointment which they figured they would adorn or offer as gifts. This was to get in good with the lord and even though it's described as bribery some see this as an important symbol. It does not mention any divine intervention in this part, these three kings just happened to see a really bright star and figured it must be the messiah. Then we are to believe that no one has any idea what the great son of God had been doing with his life from the age of 12 to 30. Really? The one and only son of the creator of everything somehow disappeared after the age of 12 and was never heard from again until he was 30. At which point he performed unbelievable miracles everywhere he went. Even what there is of his life up to 12 is practically irrelevant although he somehow becomes a teacher at this point. It is also baffling to know that Jesus had become aware that he was the son of God at this point.

So at 12 years old he knows he is the messiah yet completely goes about his business for 18 years without anyone knowing where or what he was doing. This must have made the book so much easier to complete.

There are many unbelievable stories that just don't make sense when it comes to mankind's evaluations of spirituality. All of the worlds different religions are based on absurd and sometimes impossible events. This brings us back to faith. Faith and hope are so often used together to describe a belief in something yet do not have the same definition. Hope describes the very possible, faith on the other hand means there is very little possibility. Are we to believe that God wanted to confuse Man with as much of his existence as possible all in the name of faith? Mans attempt at earthly worship of the gold calf could not go unpunished. What about the other religions that history states were also dominant in other parts of the world back then? Faith means you must ignore all other religions and Gods for God himself created these false idols to test our faith.

The other prominent religions of the world declare the same thing about Christianity,

Ignorance is bliss.

So the story continues at the age of 30, He is supported by 12 disciples as he sets out to spread the word of the Lord. He is betrayed by Judas, given up for 30 pieces of silver and crucified. The details of the story are told with exact description yet his age at the time of this is said to be around 33. How is this somehow misconstrued? It seems like the facts are based around the morals of the story and not historical accuracy. So that is a basic summary of the absurdities and contradictions of Christianity. We have gone over the fact that the world is full of many different religions. Most of which denounce all the others. How can there be so many Gods all claiming the other ones are fake? Faith, and lets stop there. Just to let what we have gone over sink in and make your own conclusions. Once again, it is not the existence of God in question but what Man has done in the name of. We are not attempting to derail anyones spirituality but to show us that believing in something should not have to come with consequences.

There is one last piece of this examination that might surprise many. The origin of Jesus is not original. All the basic facts of the birth and life of Jesus are plagiarized along with many others. This dates back to 3000 years before Jesus was said to have been born.

Horus, the Egyptian sun God, 3000 BC, was born on December 25 to a virgin named Ises Mary. Horus was visited by 3 kings who followed a star in the east and became a teacher at the age of 12. He performed miracles such as walking on water and was betrayed by one of his disciples named Typhon. Horus was crucified and after 3 days was resurrected, sound familiar? In 1200 BC, the Greek God Attis was born on December 25 to a virgin named Nana, he performed miracles was crucified and resurrected after 3 days. The Persian God Mithra was also born on December 25 to a virgin, had 12 disciples was betrayed and was resurrected after 3 days. The Indian God, Krishna, 900 BC was born to a virgin under the sign of an eastern star, performed miracles and was resurrected after 3 days. Dionysus of Greek mythology even has the same story.

This is all historically documented and available information for anyone interested in looking these facts up. Why the same story? How hard could it be to just change a few dates and stories when so much of history seems to be morphed and changed into what we want to hear and believe. Would it be less confounding if we all agreed that it's just different versions of the same God? It would make things easier but an impossible task in itself considering Man's obsessions with pride. The fact that all these other beliefs had been circulating throughout different societies around the world leads to more questions.

7 TROUBLE GOES WANDERING

The next part of the book focuses on dissent and the importance of questioning things even when we are told not to. Causing trouble is the main theme here and they really drive home the ideals of inclusion. It's important to note that it seems like some of the patients involved with this book had been let in on the mind reading alien robot gag. This is evident as it is noted every few pages that the number of people they can trust is growing. If one of the truly insane patients had brought the group to the attention of those in charge it would be taken as inane ramblings. This is what made it so important to bring those still sane on board. At this point it seemed a window for more devious schemes opened up.

Come into my parlor, said the spider to the fly! Most of us are familiar with the first line of this creepy piece of poetry. However the story is not based on conquest but vanity and flattery. Throughout the poem the spider repeatedly sings praise of how beautiful the fly's wings and eyes are. The fly at first rejects the spiders offer knowing that it would surely mean it's demise. In the end the spider's constant lip service wins over the fly's vanity and is foolishly captured by the spider. The morals here are aimed at the lure of things that build up our pride, our need for reassurance, a validation to things that make us special. If we are important we will be successful, if we are great at what we do we will have power. How about the promise of eternity? Every man in Heaven is a rich man so say your prayers. Power and control is really what this all adds up to. The greed of mankind to be powerful when being wealthy just isn't enough.

How many world leaders came into power on past ambitions to do the right things? Only to end up living inside of their own heads believing they are something they are not. Absolute power corrupts, absolutely, but this is always forgotten once power is achieved.

The spider web of religion, deception in a tangled mess of vanity and pride. The lust for power by those who deserve it least. The cults of personality that we see time after time ravaged by greed when our world leaders go unchecked. There are many who have tried to wield power without the temptations of abuse. Many have risen to the top because they saw something that was not right and decided to do something about it. Along the way they are treated differently and become gradually content with being on top. Then with power comes great responsibility and there are very few who can support this weight with honesty. Having a nation at your feet must be overwhelming. Having to make decisions on the welfare of the people who gave them the power. At that point when they are disagreed with, the abuse begins. They feel they are unfairly being portrayed by those around them. The problems mount, the commonwealth suffers and that leader is soon to be just another forgotten despot dictator in their grave.

The way this facility has empowered these religious figures and these so called doctors or psychiatrists is shameful. We will expose their greed, we will bring justice to the families of those who have disappeared behind these walls. Just as they have used the words of the Bible to keep us locked up here, we will use words to punish the guilty. The amount of money, assets and property this place has stolen can not be forgotten. Collectively, this small group of ours has lost everything we ever worked for and we can see through this charade. How much does it cost to believe? Are they paying to be saved? The importance of calling out these injustices cannot be understated. Echoing these lessons we are teaching and passing on the truth about what is going on here is exactly what we aim to accomplish. Just as the Catholic Church is the source of all of our trouble, we will reciprocate. They came looking for some easy targets in us but thats not what they got. Get the word out, rouse the mob from unrest to rebellion and we will bring chaos down upon these people. They will not see it coming.

The following is what seems to have been a template of a short letter of distress, designed to reach the outside world and maybe news outlets. It is self explanatory but I figured it best to point out there was 4 pages with the same things written. Probably to be ready to rip out and hand off to other patients who were granted visitors.

To whom it may concern:
There are several high ranking members of local institutions being held at the Holy Cross Sanitarium against our will. We have been illegally apprehended under the guise of mental or physical disabilities. All of our assets have been confiscated and our

properties and estates remanded to the Church. Patients are being subjected to horrific mind control experiments and punishment for unruly behavior is violent shock therapy or sleep deprivation torture. Please send word to any law official outside of this jurisdiction. Trust no one until then.

It takes statesmen and hooligans to complete a revolution. Some of us have to be trouble makers some of the time. In order to have someone to say that which no one else will say. Someone to question the untouchables. Someone to believe in something new and to force change. We feel like we are righting a wrong but to those in power we are trouble makers. Those of us with a talent for upsetting the apple cart.

8 CHURCH FUCKERS

No one ever wants to talk about the subject of pedophile clergy. It's in the news all the time now, can you imagine how rampant it must have been back in the mid 50's or early 60's? It is one of the most disturbing chain of events that seemed to become the norm. Another priest caught molesting children and you know it goes all the way to the top. They are the ones who send these bastards to new churches to practice because people were starting to talk. Some of them change locations several times leaving a trail of confused, frightened, messed up kids. From the Pope on down, they just keep sweeping these stories under the rug. They are not warned not to do it again, they are told not to get caught. The reason this should be brought up is the complete hypocrisy of listen, believe, follow, obey, suffer, pray, repent, abstain. Give us all of your money and we will have sex with your children. How do these disgusting freaks feel about all of this. Serving the lord all of that time and then committing acts that would surely send them straight to hell. Some don't believe in the dark, I bet those Men must eat darkness. It's known, children who are abused for extended periods often grow up to repeat those actions. Turning innocent children into raging monsters, and so on and so on. In serving the Lord, Man must sacrifice his earthly desires. Staunch Catholicism, you are married to the lord you must not seek pleasures of the flesh or something to that ideal.

Confession standards once must have kept them untouchable as the priest would know all of the parishes sins. What if someones child was an alter boy who came home with stories of being touched in bad places? The priest knows the father of the boy has been unfaithful so nothing is said. Regardless of the fact he is sworn to secrecy in all confessions it is still known. Why is it that God is always listening when you pray to him at night but you need to go through the priest to repent? They know all of the locals dirty secrets, you are even supposed to admit any sinful thoughts. It is religion that calls sex dirty, adults most pronounced need and these men have been told no. So why wouldn't they just have sex with each other? Why children? They're stuck in a monastery and children are just easy prey? Other faculty would absolutely deny any such desires? There were some confusing passages in the book that might have explained why some of them were here. We will not go into individual details on what had happened to these patients as it is un necessary, gruesome and perverse but lets just say this type of thing has gone on far too long. The information gathered in the next part of the book was graphic, disturbing and at times almost surreal. They are confessions from the far wing.

I noticed what I thought was a new young patient. At first he looked like he was in a vegetative state but I noticed him raise his head for a second as he motioned towards me. He was faking it, I could tell, he completely had his wits about him and must have come from the far wing of the hospital. Then I realized I had seen this man sweeping the floors in the main hallway yesterday. He was a custodian from the far wing and he wont be in this open group area for long, they never are. I must talk to him, we need to know what they are doing to these people. I then noticed he had a set of keys on his belt, what was he doing here? He had been sitting alone by the window when I quietly made my way over to him. I whispered, Is there anybody in there? He quickly grabbed my hand and forced a tightly folded piece of paper into it. He winked and said "Ah, the God killer! A mighty weight on your shoulders, yes? Many lives in the balance, will you do the right thing to save us, or are we not all the same in the end?" I must be getting back, He then motioned for a nurse to come get him. As they passed me by the nurse said "Be careful Godkiller, stay safe for our sake."

Just like we had thought from the start, it certainly seemed like most of the people here are totally sane and outraged at the treatment we are receiving. I walked into the washroom and quickly unfolded the piece of paper the custodian had handed me. In a crude scribbled mess, one side said Curtain brick, the other, More to come. The common areas have big bay windows and big grey curtains to cover them. When the windows are open on windy days the curtain blows around wildly and has to be kept in place. All the curtains are tied down except the one in the far corner which was near a radiator and had to be kept at distance with a cinder block. I knew what he meant. When the area was clear I went to the curtain. Under the Block was 3 tightly folded pieces of paper. A shocking confession that should have been a warning of whats to come.

I am [name removed] but just call me the custodian, I have witnessed it all and may get a chance to get out this week. Regardless of what happens to me, make sure this document stays safe as it will lead investigators to the truth. I cannot use the names of my current superiors because if this letter is found it would lead them right to me. As for the rest, they are all guilty. Everyone at the top is sworn to keep this as clandestine as possible in the name of national security. I had just finished med school and could not find a position when I was offered an assistants position at a local monastery taking care of orphans. While I was there I discovered church elders sexually abusing these orphans and in some cases alter boys. I went to the head diocese but he must have either been involved or just didn't want the truth getting out. They then framed me for stealing from the collection boxes and said they would make life very difficult if I stayed. They also told me that the guilty were to be dealt with in their own way. The optics of me being relieved of my position made it impossible for me to practice medicine in that area period. I was lucky to still have my license so I moved on vowing to one day bring the truth out to what I had witnessed. They hired me here to assist the nurses in the patients day to day ailments. I was aware that I would be dealing with the most troubled members of society but was completely unaware of their procedures and practices. I was aware they used shock treatment on patients that became violently angry and the uncontrollably spastic but the rest is was well beyond my imagination. The cruelty and inhumanity I witnessed will live with me forever. I had voiced my concerns right from the start as I was being sent patients with problems I had no idea how to deal with. I had gone from one terrible situation to something much more sinister. What has this world come to? I had brought these things to the attention my two superiors. They had told me they were well aware of what was going on and they were dealing with it. The next morning they were gone. I was told they had been called away to overlook a new project elsewhere. Ever since then I have been trying to get out. Some of these patients had been so badly drugged that they didn't even know their own names. Some had the palms of their hands burned so badly all the skin had died. They have a sleep deprivation chamber with a pedestal, if the patient falls off they get electrocuted. They are driven mad after being awake for days on end. They sedate people and place them in a big long box like a coffin. When they awake they believe they have been buried alive and are left there until the patient no longer screams for help. There were patients with holes in their heads that I had been told to sew up best as I could yet there were no brain surgeons in the hospital. They are bringing in CIA agents and training them to deal with torture by torturing them. They took men, one at a time out to the field, shackled their legs and handed them a shovel. They then told them to dig a 6 foot deep by 6 foot wide hole, they did not tell them why. A few men broke down crying, some tried to bargain and ask what it was they did to deserve this. The ones who just dig the hole are deemed loyal enough to trust. As for the criminally insane, they were trying to remove a mans stimulus to anger and violence. They end up in the calm semi vegetative state you see so often in here. They ended up removing conscience by cutting out a small piece of the brain that controls consequence and fear. This could be used for the super soldier of the future, remove fear. This was barbaric but once again, the powers that be control everything and I am trapped. I had to remove whole fingernails filled with bamboo that had been slowly driven up the patients finger with a hammer. At first, the men they had brought here were murderers, rapists and violent re offenders. Anytime they needed information, the word was out, this was a house of confession. They had extracted the whereabouts of several dead bodies and even saved a young abducted girl that was tied up in a camper. They then had prisoners brought in who would not tell the authorities where the goods they stole were hidden. From there, everything spun out of control. The army had found out what was going on just over a year ago and took over the far wing. No longer content with solving cold cases, the focus shifted to national security. Psychological torture has 4 distinct characteristics, Suffering, Infliction, deliberateness and a lack of direct physical violence. Water torture, heat torture, sleep deprivation, psychological narcotic manipulation. All of which switched to mind control after hearing some convoluted propaganda about the Russians creating an army of fight until death super soldiers. Subliminal cognitive recognition implants was a new way of introducing someones mind to an unreal fact or situation and have them fully believe it. It had been in the news recently that they had discovered G.I's returning from the Korean war had been affected by what they called Soviet brain perversion techniques. They even reported that some soldiers did not want to come home at all. The Americans had nothing to counter these rumors with and subsequently started the MK Ultra program. I was sworn to secrecy. The new occupants of the far wing did not know me apart from the 2 men I reported to when my previous superiors disappeared, and neither of them looked me in the face. As soon as they left for shift change I changed clothes and grabbed my file. I then took the place of a custodian. During my time here I have become friends with the cleaning and cooking staff and they are helping me. The staff believe I am up for vacation leave at the end of this week I will send help. The cooking and cleaning staff are on our side. They know everything, they read the documents carelessly thrown away by our Godly hosts. They overhear conversations that were not meant to be heard. You are being drugged, everyone, randomly with an untested, dangerous psychedelic narcotic called LSD. Everyone!

This was the missing piece we needed, someone who has witnessed these things first hand. Was he sane? Are we being drugged unwittingly as some sort of guinea pig experiment? Later that day, we returned from lunch to our card table to find another small tightly folded piece of paper. This one was a crude map of the far wing and where all of the security check points were located. Someone here is a step ahead of us as we had not yet even considered needing such a map. It felt like something was about to give. We told too many patients, we were not careful enough and what will they do to us if they find this book. We have not noticed feeling any different but the psychotic outbreaks of the other patients has gone up drastically.

People arguing with the walls, screaming when the lights go out, patients attacking each other. What were they trying to achieve now? Maybe because were so old and feeble they don't find us a threat or have we just not noticed being drugged? A few days later another note under the block. This one two lists of names. Under the first heading was The Guilty, which listed Doctors, nurses, clergy members, orderly's and the few army's enlisted men staffed here for security. The other heading originally had The Innocent but was scratched out and replaced with The Godkillers. If they have a list that states those who are innocent then what do they have in mind for the guilty. This obviously meant that no harm should come to the innocent. It was right then that we knew things had gone to far and had spun out of control. We have put way too many people at risk and we were no longer in control of what we started but that no longer mattered after we got the third letter.

Friends, time is short, they are expecting many new patients, therefore their staff will grow. They have people in town that are paid for spying on and turning in anyone whom may pass as emotionally disturbed, anti religious or just exhibiting odd behavior. Just like the hounds of the church during the Spanish inquisition who went out into society exposing Jews or heretics. Trust no one, the police, the elected officials, they are all being paid off.

They overheard a couple nurses talking about the cruelty, they are in rubber rooms, directly above you on the second floor. There are many up there, in straight jackets, drugged and observed. The loyal employees are getting paid extra and get bonuses for turning in potential threats. Anyone who even voices a concern at the treatments or mentions reporting whats going on are drugged in their sleep. When they wake the doctors tell them they have been under observation here for months and never were they employed here. Please don't forget them when the time comes for redemption. They took their identities away, these people that are in control are not holy, I doubt the new ones even belong to the church. The men who they've silenced are kept in the basement. In cold, dark, damp padded rooms that were put there in the event of a tuberculosis outbreak and needed to keep the dead away from the general population. It still smells of death down there these men were doctors, volunteers, orderlies, enlisted soldiers, good men that wanted to do good, this is insane. We must show them the error of their ways, we know what to do we will take it from here. Stay quiet my friends you have said enough.

What are they talking about? It says we have been spied upon and more faculty is due to arrive but they will take it from here? Something is wrong, it seems like there are fewer guards and orderlies stationed here in the main room. Have some jumped ship? More patients have started acting strange. One of the older Nurses suddenly started grabbing all of the crucifixes off the walls, stacking them in her arms and then threw them all out the window. She was screaming "stop judging me, you're not here to help, why are you staring at me?" Then she broke down weeping for possibly 30 seconds and then jerked her head up. She looked at our table and began laughing hysterically. The few who are watching us payed little attention. They were all focused on her. I doubt we will ever see her again.

My perception began to un focus and twist, colors were brighter the walls were dancing. Had I been dosed with this LSD? I went to my room and laid down, keeping my eyes closed. I had visions of leading the downtrodden and misunderstood to a better existence. To free the world of organized, conformist gatherings. A world where you can believe in whatever you want but you don't have to believe in anything. I was leading them to freedom, My ideas were manifesting. Could someone go through life without even pondering a higher consciousness? To not have a need to join a practicing collective in the need to belong. It all came full circle, our posturing as something better than the norm changed along the way. We became that which we sought to destroy. What brought us together was the need to be individual. An organized group of people who all believe that organized people all believing in the same thing is wrong. We all knew we were doing this for good, to help people. How did this happen?

9 TO KILL THE LIGHT

Accidents are what our lives are made of. What we plan doesn't mean a thing. So there may come a day where the thing you were sure you needed just becomes a catalyst for something completely different. These guys believed in what they were doing they just didn't fully understand the toll it would take. Like coming out of the dark just to kill the light. Searching for a new way to completely destroy the old. Self righteous indignation to replace ignorance and power. In denouncing religion we must then believe that our existence is finite, there will be no afterlife to plan for. We are only given one other option in evolution but what if it is neither? Could we be living a dream simulation that has somehow manifested itself as organic? Or is it just the cosmic scheme cancelling the need for chasing alternative spiritualities. Being wrongly imprisoned and then having God forced upon you every day can make one a bitter person I am sure. In saying those in power must relinquish control you might assume the person demanding justice is willing to usurp that power. You cannot simply remove someones faith without replacing it with something else, can you? After translating this all the way through, this was the place I realized why this book never saw the light of day. These last few entries were scrambled, manic, messy sentences that took me some time to fully understand. What had happened exactly will never be known but the outcome seems obvious.

I must have been given a sedative in my sleep along with the rest of our group. I woke up in a grey room with padded walls. Absolute fear, panic, I crawled over to the door and asked if there was anyone on the other side. No reply, they know about us, they're just gonna leave me here drugged and alone. Although the effects of whatever I was feeling before I fell asleep seemed to have passed. I'm not sure how long I had been asleep for but I must have been in the room close to a full day after waking. Then they came to get me. Two nurses quickly ushered me out and into a wheelchair. I was relieved to see my friends also in wheelchairs waiting in the hall. None of us knew what was going on. Both nurses had this blank stare in their eyes and one looked as if she had just been crying. I tried to ask what was going on but was interrupted abruptly with the Doctor is coming. Then to our surprise, our custodian friend appeared behind us. Friends, we have had a terrible situation unfold overnight.

He then explained what had happened. We had been sedated to keep us out of harms way. They had found out that several more faculty, army brass, CIA personnel were due to arrive next week sometime. We would then be completely outnumbered and those guilty of these crimes would escape justice. They only wanted to overpower them enough to subdue them and force them to confess to their crimes. Things got out of hand. He had only planned on sedating the officials overnight and then threatening them with the same psychological torture they had been so wrongly administering. Many knew about the plan but there were many patients that are mentally ill and trusting them to help overthrow an organization such as this was a mistake. That coupled with the fact that many of them were drugged with a psychedelic was recipe for a disaster. Another nurse had gone mad and in thinking she was drugging the faculties food, had spiked the general populations dinners. No one became aware of this until the trouble started. Now being a custodian, they had all the keys and access they needed.

The last historical comparison is that of Tomas de Torquemada. The Spanish inquisitor that mutilated, mangled and murdered many Spaniards in the name of the Lord. The fact that their were spies in town informing on anyone they could was not new. They were using sadistic torture methods in the quest of controlling the human mind, this also was nothing new.

Word got to us that the authorities in town had paid several citizens for listening in on the locals private conversations. They were listening for crazy talk, anti religious slander or anything that might give reason for a temporary evaluation incarceration at the hospital. In the late 1400's Pope Alexander VI commissioned a Man called Torquemada to deal with religious heretics and the Jewish community. It was the beginning of the Spanish inquisition. Anyone caught speaking in religious slander or practicing in Judaism were sent to a subterranean dungeon torture chamber to be dealt with. They also had what they called the hounds of the church who were sent out into the general population to spy on people. It didn't matter that many would confess right away, after all if you were being slowly burned to death on a rotisserie over red hot coals you would confess to pretty much anything. Stretched out on a rack or a lash of the whip for each denial or wrong answer.
 At first Spain needed the Jews money to help defeat the Moors and growing resurgence of Islam. By 1492 they had overseen the extinction of Judaism and had

persuaded the king and queen to force all survivors into exile. It got to the point where Torquemada no longer cared about who or what they believed. If you were sent to the inquisition you must be guilty. It was his calling to torture and mutilate in the name of God. He figured, this is not the first time the masses had faith forced upon them. Holy crusades were nothing new. The affluent believed that The Jews who did convert and renounce their faith were still treated as outcasts in society and branded with the term "Converso" Of course those who had survived were now physically disabled in gruesome ways. What is the point of all of this? Why is it that in biblical times God always had some kind of roll in great religious tragedies. Thousands of people tortured and killed, all in the name of God.

They called Torquemada "The Dark Legend" and after his reign of terror he died peacefully with his dream complete. The inquisition continued for 300 years although it had lost it's state support. They say the last victim was burned alive in 1824 yet the inquisition exists to this day under the title "The congregation for the doctrine of faith.
This still has the power to silence and excommunicate dissident Catholics. History is filled with horror stories of religious massacres and holy crusades in the name of God. Man in his pride that his God is better than the other Gods will do anything to stay on top. The idea that by torturing people they will in turn change their faith is ridiculous. Even in those times were they not to understand that these victims would confess to anything? Then go right back to praying to their original

Deity when it was all over. No one knows whats in your head but you, how could they believe they were changing thoughts when they convict you on the basis of lies to begin with? What was worse is the die hard orthodox that might have thought this a test of their true faith and refused to convert. Believing that God would save them if they remained strong and took the punishment. Faith being forced upon people was nothing new then. This type of behavior is what drives spite and division. The Gods must demand sacrifice if this type of thing went on hundreds of years with absolutely no divine intervention. No one has heard from God in 2000 odd years but before that he wouldn't shut up.

11   LUCIFERS THRONE

First big mistake was letting all the main floor patients out of their rooms. One of the patients had been nicknamed Lu for Lucifer after claims that he knew the devil personally. He had been devoutly religious all of his life and believed every word of the Bible. He also lived a life of sin, drinking, gambling, women. He figured as long as he wasn't hurting anyone and he was repenting his troubles in church on Sunday, no harm. The truth is, he was a dangerous man that should not have been part of this operation. They say Lu faked his insanity to get out of prison to stay here in a less hostile environment. The story is he had been a hard case until meeting his wife. His wife was a good person but was defiantly against the Catholic church. She had lost both parents to Tuberculosis and grew up in church run orphanages. Abused and then kicked around in foster care afterwords. She never spoke of what happened during those years. She would just say that God did not go to the same church she did. LU stopped his sins but he also stopped going to church. What would God rather have, a sinner who repents or a good man who has no faith? Apparently early on in the relationship the two would sit together in this big, fluffy, red chair drinking wine and talking about their future together. They both fit in that chair perfectly, curled up by the window. He said he wished they could just sit in that chair forever. She meant everything to him, as long as she was in his life nothing could go wrong. He was a hard working, loyal employee, kept to himself and stayed home every night with her. Somewhere along the way he says the devil started visiting him. He said the devil wanted redemption for unpaid dues. He had walked away from a life full of sin and debauchery without a scratch. He walked away from spirituality, desire and need. He said the devil was threatening to take his wife away if he would not willingly stray from what is good. He would not, he didn't believe it because the devil is nothing but trickery. The pact he had made with his wife was the only agreement he would honor. Still, he said the devil would be waiting for him, taunting him to have just one drink after work or entertaining one of the Ladies of the evening. He still would not and it began to affect him. His wife had noticed him being distant and irritable but her concerns were ignored.

 She tried to make things better, he tried to get the devil out of his life and the two tried together to make things right again. Then one day he must have gotten off work early or came home unexpectedly. She was on the big red chair in an embrace with his only close friend. The friend from work who would stick up for him and tell him not to let people push him around. His friend that he had known and trusted for years. That friend who always offered to buy him a few beers after work. That friend who always offered to pay for a lady of the evening for him. When the police arrived days later the stench inside the house was unbearable. He had called the police saying the devil had broken into his house and made a big mess. He murdered them both and kept them upright sitting in the red chair. It seems as if he had kept changing his wives clothing, brushed her hair and even attempted feeding her. At the same time he was insulting and ridiculing his ex friend, blowing smoke in his face and telling him how stupid he looked sleeping upright. Bragging to a deadman that he had won back his wives affections. How he could stand the smell in that house is amazing yet he sat beside them talking to them for days. He said as long as she was sitting in the red chair the devil could not get to him. Was Lu insane or did he just live through something so tragic and absurd that all sanity had temporarily escaped him?

I suppose after days of rigor mortis her appearance had changed enough that he no longer recognized her. He only saw Lucifer when he looked at the chair. He was kept in a rubber room for the first 3 months and then let out in a straight jacket, at first. He had been making progress here until the new staff arrived. When they found out his past he was one of the first to be put through the new torture practices for mind control and extracting information. Lu had an ally who let him out, a few others went to check the security posts.

 The doctor began crying, He then just said, "It was not meant to be this way." We later found out exactly what had happened. The custodian had put a sleeping agent in the night securities coffee supply. Only those 4 officers are heavily armed. However at such a strong dose they must have passed out while doing rounds. The gateway to the far wing was opened and the security guards were asleep on the floor. It was a bloodbath, they cut off two of their heads and hung the other two. We went down to the basement to free the male Doctors and as we were leaving we passed by the laundry rooms. This is where the back door leading to the cliffs was located. They dragged the men in charge out back at gun point and made them get in the sacks. One by one they tipped them over the cliff. There were a handful of sadistic nurses that were rounded up and brought to the electro shock rooms. They were fried to death. This was not at all what we had planned for, we only wanted to expose the guilty. We were in shock at what had been told to us but we had to se the far wing and what was going on down there. As we turned the hallway corner we saw the first trails of blood. Then more as we passed through the security check point. The two heads that had been removed from the soldiers were perched on top of the railing posts that held a dividing rope. The sound of manic laughter and screaming echoed down the hallway, how did this all happen? They had somehow torn an arm off one of the nurses and left it with the phone in the front office off the hook and in it's hand. Written in blood across from the front doors were the words " monster factory " We will all hang for this if we cant get away from here. We have no access to our banks and there was maybe 6 or 7 cars parked out front. Not nearly enough to pack everything up and disappear. We needed to reach someone outside of this district to somehow come and extract the innocent. Problem is that now it seems none of us are.

We removed the nurses arm from the front desk phone and hung up the receiver. The phone began ringing instantly, I answered with just "Hello, hospital." I must have sounded like someone else as a deep gravelly voice began speaking to me in a furious tone. He said "

Your patients have somehow been getting the word out as to whats going on in there. Pack up everything that could be used as evidence and destroy all of the test drugs. I want no sign of the armed forces ever being in that building. They are sending authorities from the capital, get the hell out of there. As of now this operation never existed and we have never been in contact, do you understand? Get out of that area all together, go back to your home town or to a relatives and lay low until this all blows over." I quickly said "Yes sir, will do!" and hung up.

We had one chance to get out of this mess but considering many of the patients were still loose in the building doing who knows what, any coordinated effort would be tough. We made our way through the halls gathering all the patients who were still of sound mind and were willing to stop and listen. There was a lot of mess to clean up but luckily for us it was contained to 3 areas only. The first was the front hall and the 4 dead armed forces personnel. It looked like they were originally attacked with surgical instruments, knives, scalpels who knows. Their bodies were perforated and covered in blood. The 2 headless guards were perched upright in their chairs. One at the security desk, who had its arms outstretched with a pen in one hand and the other was wrapped around a coffee mug. The other headless guard was in a chair facing the front doors. Propped up with a coat rack in behind his jacket forcing his arms outward. Feet crossed in crucifix pose, they were not satisfied in just killing them.

On either side of the propped up soldier were the 2 decapitated heads sitting on posts that were connected by a thick red rope. There were a handful of these posts that ran down the hallway outside of the examination rooms. Chairs lined the walls for an express line to the nut house. A decapitated corpse in a slouching crucified position flanked by 2 heads skewered on brass posts. The other 2 soldiers were hung off flagpoles on either side of the foyer. The poles were only 10 feet off the ground. These guards were not hung they were choked to death.Their necks did not break, they were slowly asphyxiated. Eyes bulging out of their sockets in a final frozen gasp for life. Black electrical chords tied tightly around the tops of their throats. The armless nurse lay on the floor before them. Heavily drugged, imprisoned and abused psychiatric patients are capable of madness. Did the people in charge not think, that doing these tests in a place like this may not be a great idea? Normally, subjects are screened and compensated for volunteering for new drug studies. Why do it in a hospital full of all kinds of dangerous individuals? The bodies were bundled up, taped and dragged down the hall to the laundry chute. The bodies would then only be 30 feet from the cliffs in the basement. We put every mop in the place to use and got rid of the broken furniture. We then had to clean up the chapel. We had first thought the priests wrists had been slit but that wasn't the case. All 3 men had holes drilled through the palms of their hands symbolic of Jesus wounds or stigmata. Hanging from the altar cross we noticed another set of sadistic deformities. One of them had his eyes removed. The next had ears sliced off and the third, missing his tongue. See no evil, hear no evil, speak no evil. We got the bodies down and wrapped them up like the others.

Tossing mutilated priests down laundry chutes, what redemption is this? At this point a few of the staff that had been silenced and thrown into rubber rooms were starting to come too. We explained what had happened and put everyone to work. Either mopping blood or just searching the hospital for lost stragglers. The last major disaster area was the basement experiment rooms. Nurses fried to death, one had the reflex gag that keeps patients from swallowing their tongues rammed down her throat. Head covered in electrodes, blood pouring out of her eyes and ears. The horrible stench of a Bar B Q gone wrong. A heap of dead bodies lay on the floor beside the table. We had to find out who was still armed with the guns that had been taken from the sleeping guards. Then it dawned on one of us that this was all the work of Lu. Posing his cheating wife and ex friend for days after they had died at his hands.

A few of the remaining bodies were put into the burlap and tossed over. The rest buried in the side yard. The Vultures were out in full force, sensing the obvious death that had gone on just above. There was also dinner waiting, washed up between 2 rocks below. The ones who did not put up a fight peacefully stepped into the sacks. Begging for forgiveness and claiming they were only following orders. They were dragged to the edge as the Blocks were thrown over. The sheer force pulled them down right behind. One of the sacks must have torn open on a jagged rock and freed the corpse. We made sure to toss the remaining dead straight down into the bay. The tide was coming in and the edge of the cliff was a good 40 feet out over the water. It should keep them out of sight for the time being. We were mopping and scrubbing the basement areas when we suddenly heard a crash, then another. We stopped everything and looked out back toward the noise.

 We instantly saw 2 figures fall past the rock face and a voice yelling ""God has tentacles" The sound of the crashing was 2 wheelchairs being thrown off the roof of the hospital. Emery and Dunstal cleared the cliffs edge while falling, their wheelchairs didn't. The two had been making home made booze again with fruit rinds and sugar. The 2 made a suicide pact but over estimated how far they could actually jump in wheelchairs. They both rolled as fast as they could right off the roof but did not even clear the veranda. The wheelchairs bounced once and came crashing down below. There is a gradual slope on the awning above the deck, they must have thought they would be airborne from the momentum, The 2 old men rolled off the side and directly straight down into the bay. While cleaning the laundry room we came across a set of instructions for disposing of linens and clothing. Anything soiled so badly it could not be properly disinfected or items possibly infected by trans-missable diseases. The burlap was not for disposing unwanted patients after all. Upon leaving the basement we ran into Lu and a few other patients that had been searching for the last few guilty personnel. We approached them with caution and before we could ask, Lu said "It's OK, I did what you could not, you will be safe now," He seemed completely calm, almost like nothing happened. He told us there were a handful of good helpful people locked up in the staff lounge. They had made sure the small group of staff that had not been involved in any wrong doing were safe. He said there were nurses who gave him comfort and had empathy to the situation. He was of sound mind, yet he was a cold blooded, calculating murderer.

We were responsible for much of this, we told them they should stand up and fight for the truth. Lu paused long enough to hear what we had to say. There were no army personnel coming and the mind control experiments had been cancelled, at least in that location they were. Lu and his cohorts had all the weapons that had been seized from the front. They had planned on ambushing any new faculty due to arrive and then barricade themselves in until they had a plan for a clean escape. We told them about the phone call and that there was federal level officials, police and probably the press due to arrive within the next 24 hours.

 After explaining the situation Lu agreed to help get the remaining sane patients to gather in the common room. As there was no more need for killing at that point, the weapons were all rounded up and hidden. Lu started off alone down the hall then stopped. He said " Sorry for the mess but Hell is waiting for me" A gun went off and Lu hit the floor. One more headless corpse to dispose of. After all the madness that filled his life it should not have come as a surprise. He must have held onto one of the guards pistols and planned it the whole time. The sinner who had a God to a saint without one. He was right though, he did what we could not. It must have been God's will, everything happens for a reason. Mutilating the guilty in ritual pose. He fully believed he was righteous and on a mission to right the wrongs that go on here. Sometimes the righteous have to behave evil in order to defeat evil. We mopped and disinfected the hallways. We then made sure the mentally ill patients that were still wandering the halls got back into their rooms. We removed all the files belonging to those who were killed and removed all the brick and burlap. Files belonging to those in charge were plagiarized and replaced with ours putting our custodian doctor in charge of the whole operation.

We knew who we could trust after all the hours of teaching anyone who would listen. The building was cleaned, the blood mopped up and every precaution taken. That night a group of patients that had been wrongly incarcerated along with some helpful staff took the car keys to a few of the vehicles and safely got out of town. The safe in the front office had been opened and deeds to properties, life savings and estate claims were returned to their rightful owners. Sure enough a group of elected officials from the capital arrived the next morning. To our relief no local authorities had accompanied them. The rumors of everyone in town being paid off for their services must have been true. We sat at our usual table playing cards, watching, hearts pounding, wondering if there was something we missed. The custodian gave the visitors a short tour and upon inspection found nothing criminal or unusual going on.

We could have gotten away that afternoon but by that
point why would we want to leave?
The inmates are running the asylum.

                        THE END

12 THE FORGONE CONCLUSION

To start with, My guess is that the book must have been hidden away that very day. They could have gotten rid of it or burned it but probably wanted the story to be told eventually. Were they responsible for what had happened? There must have been much weight on their shoulders directly afterwords. They tried to teach everyone to think outside the box. To question all that seems wrong and fight back against all oppressors. The book would certainly make them seem guilty of inciting the riot. Did they get away with it? Did they leave the hospital ? No one knows, unless there is another book stashed up high in those rafters we will never know. Read into it however you would like, criticism of religious institutions is nothing new. It's chaos that is guaranteed to affect those not expecting it. Whatever helps you sleep at night, religion, sex, drugs, success, go for it, you deserve a break. Think for yourself and believe in freewill. Remember you do not have to agree with the world. Idle hands do the devils work, the story herein may be considered evil and blasphemy yet it was all based on the search for Good. No one seems to know what questions to ask, some want to know who, some want to know what. Maybe the sky is deceiving and theres nothing up there. Faith poses more questions then it answers. It is not the aim of telling people what to believe, or changing anyones mind. The idea is simply to question the things in our life that do not make sense to us. We don't have to be locked up in a hospital to notice the things that are not right. Words are important and are examined very closely these days. Whatever it is that you're saying, make sure you say it right, for the world is out there ready to prove you wrong. Be weary of what you wish for, you might just get it.

Punky Weirdo

13 THE GODKILLERS HANDBOOK

1/ The Holy Sanitarium

The Inter-galactic, Telepathic, Octogenarian, Alien, Robot, False messiah hunters.
Collective undercover
From a grey world with walls of rubber
Origin re-discovered

2/ God Has Tentacles pt 1.

God has tentacles, but he's not an Octopus,
He beats up prostitutes, He's always sleeping on the bus.
God has tentacles, His teeth are green and cracked,
He lies about his age, He's trying to forget his past.

3/ Some Irrational Catalyst.

Stay geared towards the exceptional, and leave the average behind
From where came this light? Distant voices in the night
that tend to stay right by your side.
Because it keeps you warm. shelter from cold and storm
helps you to climb the hill.
Just a thought away, the first hit of the day
to hold, to get my fill, the fixations thrill.
I would never stray, no more habits to trade
but then you go away, and leave me alone again
halfway up the hill, take away my thrill.
It might be dumb luck, but either way your bound to get fucked,
better often than over, better up for free

those of us in need, for a push to succeed, to get up the hill.
And the Devil couldn't figure out the latch on the gate at the side of the house,
don't let him out back, he's just wants a familiar place to hang out.
Then he follows me around. Our souls in direst jeopardy because of rock and roll
and the sex and drugs and constant excuse for losing control, we just sold our souls
Feather ink and scroll

4/ The Unseen Illusion.

I once was paranoid, they took me away
They took me away because I was paranoid
I was paranoid because I thought that they were coming to take me away
and when they took me away, they could not occupy my brain. Obsessive fixation, frustration and eventually submission
then hopefully salvation, this aimless situation void of any direction
may conjure inspiration, theres just no more time for confession
Light for the blind, branded insane by their crooked design
eyes to the sky, there's something up there its just so hard to find.
What is it that blinds them? I think I know, they think they know things,
they think they see things, they think they know what no one else knows.

So bless me and save this indifferent soul, these late
hour breakdowns
could not be controlled, it's an arduous task I have taken
on, this mission
to exert the needed energy to channel my ambition.
Driving the stake, the illusion we don't see is about to
break
A faith to forsake, one small careless secret becomes a
killing mistake.
The secret is known by very few and spoken of even
rare,
behind gold doors they whisper the truth, "the game
cannot be played fair"
There's reason why the story could never be sold
kept hidden through the ages, the truth remains untold
for if this illusion is ever taken away, the horror of reality
would render us all insane.
So will it to be, just who the fuck do they think they
deceive
control and greed, and blind faith in a story no one would
ever believe.
How the fuck can there be so many Gods? when each
God claims
that they're the only one. They made very natural desire
a sin, only the wicked have fun.
Welcome to the destination of the abandoned, we are at
war with what is.
We gambled our souls, we didn't understand.
Trapped here by our own devices.
The moon has begun to outshine the sun,
nothing times everything amounts to one.

5/ God Has Tentacles II

God has tentacles, He's got plans for the meek
He's been wandering for eternity, He only smokes the finest weed
God has tentacles, A real prick if he don't get his way
the challenge of the hunt is gone, there are no dragons left to slay.   He's got Satan held at bay.

6/ Trouble Goes Wandering.

Come into my parlor, this time the fly had the upper hand
There's a problem that must be faced, the exceptions have been erased
A tangled web falls in a storm, and the spider is washed away
Trouble gone wandering today.
Conform and serve me blindly, as you starve and die in the streets
it's tomorrow's pollution, there is no solution
unrest grows to a dangerous height, soon just another forgotten man in his grave
Trouble's gone wandering again.
I am the troublemaker, shit disturber, I've got the dirt
I am obnoxious, profound statement, I come from where words hurt.
unshackled from the chains of faith, what does it cost to believe?
rouse the masses from unrest to rebellion and bring chaos to those who deceive.

Pay to pray, pay to be saved, this hole I dig wont be my grave

there's trouble in my shadow it's always been that way, I
don't pray.
Bottles fill the hallways, roaches in the sink, trouble's
been following me around again
it's an acute psychotic link.
Show me to the easy way and I will turn it into a
problem,
show me to the problem I will fuck it up worse
so don't bother asking me to solve them.
Still the voices egg me on, the decisions that I make
always somehow seem to be wrong in every step I take.
Some don't believe in the dark, some know the dark all
to well,
There's trouble in my shadow, it drags me through Hell,
straight through Hell.

7/ Church Fuckers.

Repent, Ye wretched lost souls. Repent, you will burn in
that hole.
One last thing before I put my faith back on the shelf,
these men in the churches should stop fucking little
boys.
and just go fuck themselves.
Maybe I'm just unholy, maybe I was born wrong
but I fell through a crack in reality, we've been deceived
all along
so get on with your struggle, you have something new to
fear,
the lord doesn't have your back anymore, and no one
gives a fuck around here.
Listen, Believe, Follow, Obey, Suffer, Pray. Repent.
Abstain.
Whorehouses of the holy, Nativity blaspheme

They've been fucking in the church for years and they've kept us on our knees.
While it's become all to common to turn our backs on someone an arms length away
much like this system in which I'm forced to belong, I am broken, I am in pain.

8/ God Has Tentacles III

God has tentacles, He's got one disappointing Son
He brags about his fucking globe, he thinks he owns everyone
God has tentacles, he's married to a barnacle
his glory never yields, he lives in a burned out car in an empty field.

9/ to kill the light

There may come a day, when what you thought that you wanted
was no longer be there to have, there's no divine right
I came out of the darkness, a sole purpose to kill the light
Existence finite, something non organic, a generating source of life
The cosmic scheme will booster reality into the dream
the conscious world aint what it seems.
Can you see through invisible veils, don't you dare tell them that you can Dogmatic justification to avoid guilt, the self righteous speak of things they don't understand.
No one has the right, there are no exceptions, to tell someone what to believe,
enlightenment comes from open minds, ungovernable and free.

10/ Torquemada's Vision.

I no longer give a good God damn, to who or what you believe

my calling is to torture and maim, from the screams of the wicked I feed.

But is this really the work of the lord? for I feel human no more

and the mangled souls that leave this place are not the first to know faith by force.

The privileged affluent will soon understand, with this dark legend heresy ends

They'll convert or face the hounds of the church, they'll believe or they'll be condemned

11/ Lucifers Throne.

Mouth wide open, hands in his lap, head tilted back, kinda looks dead, he just sits there.

Somebody sleeping in my red chair, he's been passed out all day long

looks kinda stupid just sitting there, passing out upright just seems wrong.

He just sits there, nowhere he's gotta be, twitching once in a while

I've been blowing smoke in his face all day long, he sometimes seems to smile.

Why would you say it was, how could you think it was, why do you believe it was,

what makes you so sure? I knew it must have been him sitting there, cause I knew it wasn't her

12/ The Forgone Conclusion.

We are the downtrodden. the left behind, the all inclusive, racially blind
if you don't fit in anywhere else, you will fit in here.
These streets are lonely and unforgiving, make no mistake its no easy living,
but when there's nothing to lose there is nothing to fear.
They kneel and they pray, the morally enslaved, all desire abstained, all will restrained
finding solace in being one with the divine. {when times were bad jesus sent you a sign}
Some coincidental bush of fire, you give it all, your money, your life and your soul,
to the Billion dollar brainwashing cult that has one simple goal-control.
So enlighten yourselves, come live to win, be proud of your faults, embrace your sins
with tales we tell of the hell we've all lived through.
The politicians preach, the clergy will judge, the police have lawyered up now that children carry guns. Maybe Punk rock is the right thing to do.

13/ God Has Tentacles IV

Read into this what you will, it's chaos aimed at the quiet still
the comfortable bed doesn't come from greed, so habitual dependency fills the need
But when artificial joy runs short, the game of life becomes a vicious sport
fuck the world, til it fucks you back, just don't do jesus it's worse than crack

With the devil in these idle hands, the questions no one seems to understand
Who is what? and how and why? fools to believe in the deceiving sky
Bendeco manifesto, The Godkillers handbook, incognito this message has more than one disguise,
you better wake the fuck up and open your fucking eyes.
Tell me how do you define being free?
I don't follow them I follow me, don't let anyone or anything stand in your way,
and live without restrictions til the end of your days
God has tentacles, He's been trying to warn us all,
He offers no apologies, the sky is about to fall.

All music and lyrics written and performed by the Bendecos
THE BENDECOS ARE:
Dale Gallagher-Bass and vocals
Martin Luud-guitars and production
Jeff Smith-Drums
Kevin Smith-guitar and lead vocal

Additional guitars by Kam Price and backing vocals.

This book is dedicated to everyone who dares call me a friend.

A big thank you to a great bunch of people, Dan "Shennan" Aldred, Coiler C, Bowser T, Jamie E, Johnny, Sue and Layla, Boy R D, Carrots, Shatsky, Lala,

Christine, Nikki, Pam, Beth, Suzy, Shelly, Jenna R.I.P, Terry, Veikko, Tyrone, Stampy, Rob W, Philthy L, Charlie, Bud life delivery, Myles [shirts], Taelor, Dirty bird, Knifehammer, Random killing, BFG's. Black Donnelleys, Punching nuns, ELE, Shootin Blanx, 3 easy payments.
And a big apology to all I forgot, I am way past deadline to get this to my publisher. Always the oblivious procrastinator.

Additional guitars and backing vocals by Kam Price.

www.ingramcontent.com/pod-product-compliance
Lightning Source LLC
Chambersburg PA
CBHW031349160726
47993CB00002B/896